mags and comics of (now, sadly) yesteryear. In a surreal way, *The
Big Yaroo* is the meaning of life.' **Danny Denton**, author of *The
Earlie King and the Kid in Yellow*

'Hilarious, touching and terrifying, *The Big Yaroo* charts the final, geriatric disintegration of a perpetual childhood. Tormented and cruel insights cut open like diamonds a narrative woven out of more than half a century's worth of monstrous and pathetic dreaming. The most distinctive voice in Irish literature has returned: Francie Brady rides again!' **Oisín Fagan**, author of *Nobber*

'Dark, irreverent, sharp and energetic – Pat McCabe's exceptional gifts remain unparalleled.' **Nicole Flattery**, author of *Show Them a Good Time*

'Pat McCabe, the generous genius of contemporary Irish letters, catches us up with Francie Brady, an old man now, but still a thrill in these days of digital babble.' **Henry Glassie**, author of *The Stars of Ballymenone*

'Any reader who, like me, has been moved, changed, by the experience of reading *The Butcher Boy* will feel impelled towards this novel by a character who, many decades of incarceration and anti-psychotic drugs later, is still the Francie Brady that, joyously, unbearably, we recognise.' **Ross Raisin**, author of *God's Own Country*

PATRICK McCABE

NEW ISLAND

THE BIG YAROO
First published in 2019 by
New Island Books
16 Priory Office Park
Stillorgan
County Dublin
Republic of Ireland

www.newisland.ie

Hardback ISBN: 978-1-84840-746-6
Paperback ISBN: 978-1-84840-741-1
eBook ISBN: 978-1-84840-742-8

Typeset by JVR Creative India
Cover and handwritten notes designed by Philip Barrett, www.blackshapes.com
Printed in Poland by Introkar, www.introkar.com

New Island received financial assistance from The Arts Council (An
Comhairle Ealaíon), Dublin, Ireland.

New Island Books is a member of Publishing Ireland.

For Daniel Bolger, with thanks.

Contents

Chapter 1	What Is Exhibit X?	1
Chapter 2	Philately	4
Chapter 3	The Two Blanchflowers	17
Chapter 4	The Island of Cuba	25
Chapter 5	New York City, 1947	31
Chapter 6	Mysterious People	37
Chapter 7	Big Day in Annagreevy	49
Chapter 8	The Picnic at Blackbushe	56
Chapter 9	The Loneliness of *Emmerdale Farm*	60
Chapter 10	Niki Lauda	67
Chapter 11	The Russians, the Russians, the Russians Aren't Coming	81
Chapter 12	Teatime with Tommy	88
Chapter 13	Leaves	97
Chapter 14	Cat's Eyes Cunningham	104
Chapter 15	The Angel of Dresden	119
Chapter 16	Terminal	133
Chapter 17	A Song of Praise	175
Chapter 18	Throw Your Voice	184
Chapter 19	Pansy Potter the Strongman's Daughter	192
Chapter 20	The Big Breakout	205

Chapter 1
What Is Exhibit X?

That, for me, remains the big question of today – just what is it, Exhibit X?

But I believe I may have found the answer.

Which is as follows: John Brody, science reporter of the *Daily Newsflash*, goes to the village of Tolworth and discovers that the people there are influenced by a sinister machine – yes, you've guessed it:

Exhibit X.

Brody learns that Exhibit X is persuading the townsfolk to make copies of itself. These copies are seen as everyday objects – statues, ornaments, etc. – by those in its power.

Brody hurries back to London to report this disturbing 'headline story', only to find a copy of Exhibit X on the editor's desk.

So I'd say that gave him a bit of an old jolt, wouldn't you?

Ah yes.

There's no doubt about it.

You know, these days, whenever I find myself looking back over the years – reviewing the various ups & downs of my life, as they say, I am always reminded of the number of people who have come up to me from time to time and said to me: Frank, what is the situation – who, of all the performers that you've seen over the years would you say is your all-time absolute & unqualified favourite, eh?

& which is a question to which I have always given the exact same never-changing answer – beyond all shadow of a doubt, Mr Jack Palance, wry star of *City Slickers* & fabled presenter of the legendary television programme, *Believe It or Not*.

Which, if you're one of the one-and-a-half people in the world who have never happened to get around to viewing it, I suggest you get on your phone this minute & download as many series as you can.

For, beyond all shadow of a doubt, it is just about the most enjoyable show you are ever going to see.

Believe It or Not, ha ha ha!

With no end of bewildering & astonishing facts right there at your disposal – I mean, where else are you likely to discover that jellyfish in one day can eat ten times their body weight?

Or that jaywalking in Singapore carries a six-month term?

Truly amazing.

&, at the end of the day, every bit as good, if not better, than a lot of the other stuff available to citizens in this so-called digital age.

Such as David Attenborough, for example.

I mean, how many colouredy fish can you watch?

Because after a while, they all seem the same.

Exactly what I say in my TV column, which I've only just finished this morning, after working on it nearly the whole blooming night.

But it's done now, anyway, so no complaints there.

& I have to say that it's definitely looking good, probably the best article yet, I would think.

Ever since I started work on the magazine, I spend a great deal of time here in my office, always discovering amazing facts such as the above.

Not to mention the truth about Exhibit X, as I say.

Initially I had intended it just as a kind of amusement or pastime, but in more recent times have begun to consider that it might be something much more important. Joomag is the programme I use.

& which is described in the online ad as:

'An easy access publishing platform for everyone, designed for heterogeneous interactive content creation.'

I genuinely never thought, at this stage of my life, that I'd be in a position to discover my true vocation.

But there you are – yes, here he comes, the man who finally blew the whistle on Exhibit X.

I've more or less done all the artwork myself – with a little assistance from my associate Ricky Shabs, if you could call him that.

Because I'll tell you this – send out Shabs on the smallest mission, even to get you a Kit Kat, & you'll be lucky if you set eyes on the frigger by nightfall.

But talking about Kit Kats reminds me of a topic I was only writing about last week – casually at first, & then it ending up covering well over fourteen pages, which is often the way with *The Big Yaroo*.

Chapter 2
Philately

Sweets, you just can't be up to them.

I devoted a complete whole column to them this morning.

'Lucky Lumps of 1963', the piece was called.

Other confections popular during that particular period would have included another perennial favourite, the tasty Chiclet and not forgetting His Majesty Mr Choffee, Clarnico-Murray's world-famous brand.

Which, as the name suggests, was a mixture of warm melted caramel covered in a delicious coating of the yummiest-tasting choc.

But they have long since disappeared off the market, so far as I know.

& which I have to say is a pity.

Still, that's enough about confections now, for after all I have already written 15,000 words, so I think it's time to give it a rest.

Anyway, I need a bit of fresh air – because it can get quite stuffy here in the publishing world ha ha.

So it's off now with The Frank for his traditional afternoon ramble.

During the course of which, hopefully, I won't have the misfortune to encounter that long-nosed interfering bastard Corrigan.

He's been here for over a thousand years.

Well, maybe not quite – but he does look like something some unsuspecting farmer might uncover on his land, from round about the time of the Bronze Age.

A lot of people who have passed through here have been convicted of all sorts of really quite unspeakable crimes, including myself.

With some either shooting people or shoving the prongs of a graip through their chest, like Mattie McCrann who's out in Portrane now.

Fizzbag was built in 1852, and like it says in the big fancy brochure they have printed about it, its Victorian features can be observed in every aspect, blah blah blah thirty-four acres of well-groomed lawns behind an eighteen-foot wall south of Dublin City.

Not that you could call it a mental hospital now, or an asylum for the criminally insane or anything – not really.

Seeing, like McCrann, as most of the residents have been shifted out to North Dublin, by the water.

& where they all, I'm happy to say, appear to have settled in well.

As a matter of fact, I had a phone call from Mattie only just this morning.

Over the moon, he was.

About the food and the way they've been treated, the whole lot.

–What more could anyone want? he says, Frank – eh? Answer me that! The best of materials has gone into the building of it, and it right slap bang by the side of the sea. Did you know that there's even an ultra-modern gym? I'll send you a couple of snaps just as soon as I get settled. Ah boys, but it's a terror all the same the way things change – to think that only a week or two ago we were stuck in that auld dump where you still are, and the golden strand just out there beyond your window. I'll bet you're fucking sorry you didn't agree to come now, are you Frank?

They're always at me – with Dr Cecil being the absolute worst, to forget about Fizzbag Mansions and pack my bags and become one of the 'Portrane Team'.

& part of me, I know, would definitely like to.

But I'm sorry to have to say that, in the end, it's always the same – at the very last minute I decide to change my mind.

& come right back in to my room here in Fizzbag and start unpacking my cases once more.

As if it's my very first day on the block, like it was in 1963.

&, you know, I really would like to able to say that I miss them so much, Mattie McCrann and all my old colleagues & that sometimes it can really prove difficult to get through the day without them.

But that, I'm afraid, would be a total pack of lies – particularly where that old Mattie is concerned, always coming up to you & asking you questions.

–I say there, Frank! That's all you ever hear when poor old McCrann is around, there's something I've been meaning to ask you, Frank!

Ah no, I'm sorry to have to admit it, but there's powerful peace with McCrann having gone vamoose – even though he's a thoroughly decent chap.

Unlike some of the scuts that you'll find around here.

Or used to.

With the great advantage being that now they're all gone I've been pretty much appointed Cecil's loyal second-in-command, granted permission to wander as I will, provided of course I don't scale the wall.

Not that I have any notion of escaping, at least not right at this very moment.

Seeing as I'm way too busy to be bothered – what with the magazine & everything.

Speaking of which, I was thinking of including a showbiz column – or do you think that these days I would be wasting my time? I mean, it's not as if there isn't enough out there already, with no end of gibberish about celebrity chefs & food & drink, not to mention *X Factor* Cowell & c'mon and we'll all enter *Dancing with the Stars.*

Maybe, though, an article about some forgotten pop idol from long ago in the mists of time.

Such as Terry Dene, perhaps – I wonder did you ever hear of him – kind of the Cliff Richard that never was, I suppose.

Or Tuesday Weld.

I came upon a load of stuff about her there the other day, completely by accident.

& must have spent six hours reading it.

Apparently, she was born in NYC in 1943 and began acting as a child. Her performance in *Rally 'Round the Flag, Boys!* impressed executives at 20th Century Fox who signed her to a long-term contract. One of her most successful shows at Fox was *Return to Peyton Place*, in the part played by Hope Lange in the original.

Hope Lange? I remembered her.

Because I used to always watch *Peyton Place* through the window of the front room in Nugents'.

Before it all went wrong and all the rest of it.

After that, Weld was cast in a role in *Lord Love a Duck* along with Roddy McDowall, Harvey Korman and Ruth Gordon.

The film became a cult success.

Which doesn't surprise me – not in the least.

Because the more I think about Tuesday Weld – I mean, what a smasher!

So I downloaded all the pictures I could find, even from the most obscure television series, and stuck them up all over the office.

With the result that you could hardly see yourself for Tuesday Welds.

But I mean, I'm sure there must be an appetite for interesting facts about people like her – out there, among the kids I mean.

Who must be getting fed up with the likes of Simon Cowell & Beyoncé & Rihanna & all the rest of them by now.

Because I can tell you this – I know I fucking am.

Maybe a little piece about the old-time foods Cowell liked.

But then, when you think about it, they might just as quick turn around, laugh their holes off.

& say – what on earth is he blathering about now?

That poor old Frank – Fizzbag Mansions is still the place for him, just make sure & keep him there.

Yeah, I reckon they could just as easily say that.

OK then – what about Michael Parkinson, maybe something about him?

Yes, a light-hearted feature, perhaps concerning the subject of the one & only talk-show champion of the seventies, yep, good old Parky – for when it comes to it, there wasn't one to touch him.

& I always made sure to make it my business not to miss him, each & every Saturday night.

Nine-thirty on the dot, snug as a bug in my telly lounge chair watching as the spotlight swept & picked out Mike, grinning as he swung and tented his fingers.

I'm still a devil for the telly, you know.

Sometimes I'll watch maybe six or seven programmes.

& which is why I find it more or less great being alive these days, what with Amazon Prime, Netflix & all the rest.

You could watch a dozen series in a row if you wanted, & there's no one here that's going to stop you.

Welcome to the world of the internet, I say.

Where, anything you want, you can get it on eBay – man alive, the stuff that's on there for sale!

I'm going to include a free gift with the mag.

That should soon shift a couple of copies – I'll advertise it all over the net.

Ladies & gentlemen, welcome to the pages of The Big Yaroo, *complete with our readers' own special free gift –* The Magic Spinner! *Cracker-Banger!* or whatever.

***

Maybe, even, a special book of stamps.

On second thoughts – don't be talking to me about them.

Because I think I've had more than a bellyful.

Although, to be honest, whenever I was young, I couldn't hear enough about Monaco, the Gold Coast & all those other places that were famous for printing spectacular stamps – indeed, anything at all to do with philately, as my father called it.

As a matter of fact, I always had four or five albums on the go at once.

All stuffed to the gills with hundreds of magnificent, serrated rectangles and squares, steamed off envelopes from everywhere you could think of around the world.

With humungous triangles, squares and diamonds to be collected from countries whose names you could just about pronounce and no more.

Inavunky, Blaggo-Blaggo, all these different principalities – most of which were ruled by the British, with King George on the top where Queen Victoria had once been – but without his body, just George's head looking tasty in gold leaf.

Another good place to collect from was Tanganyika, I remember.

Boy, did those folks know how to decorate an envelope.

With huge big geometric shapes displaying images of what you could only describe as Paradise – with no end of toucans and parakeets and beautiful, steaming palm trees, swaying beneath the blue, limitless dome of the sky.

–As good as a hundred and fifty Bundorans! Wee Pat Casey used to say.

And that's exactly what I used to think it would be like – & which was why I sent away for my book of approvals.

Where – if you accepted the terms – you could find yourself collecting no end of 'philatelic wonders' all ready to be dispatched 'to your door' in an enormous transparent cellophane bag.

With the only obligation being that you had to send them a letter with your signature on it and make sure & promise to return the chequebook-sized booklet containing 32 pages of 'Conditional Approvals'.

& just so long as you made sure to inform your parents of just what it was, exactly, you were doing.

In which case, providing you abided by that one essential condition then you could order all the stamps you wanted, fill up your house with them till it burst.

And which sounded like a very good proposition to me, I have to say.

Yes, absolutely.

Terms I considered most 'excellent & reasonable', on offer from the Bridgnorth Philatelic Services, from somewhere far far away – Warwickshire, in the United Kingdom.

The booklet itself was also an attractive little item with a shiny purple metallic cover and a picture of Queen Victoria right up there, looking sombre in the corner.

With her soft pudgy hands like little animals there on her lap. 'The World-Famous Penny Black', it read, front, worth ££££££'s.

That, however, was just the beginning.

Because, when you read on down, this is what you found – with more

&

more

&

more,

after that.

PLUS the 1953 Cape Triangular Facsimile (originals worth £45) plus a genuine dealer's mixture of 200 unsorted stamps (catalogued over 30/-), all ABSOLUTELY FREE! Just ask to see our new approvals and enclose 3d. for postage (please tell your parents).

Buy this, buy that, everything said.

I mean – just how persuasive is that to a ten-year-old boy?

So, to tell you the truth, I'd have bought the lot – exploding cushions, x-ray glasses, you name it.

But, as my father, God rest him, used to always say – never buy anything unless you have the money.

Neither a borrower nor a lender be.

No. Never buy anything unless you can absolutely one hundred per cent afford it.

This is what it said: that you were allowed to hold on to the approvals for a fortnight – and maybe that might explain why I became complacent.

Because when you're ten, fourteen days is a complete eternity.

I'll send them back tomorrow, I kept saying.

& definitely did mean it.

But then what happened? I went and lost the fuckers.

& as soon as I realised, tore the place upside down.

Without success.

& then gradually, both in the day and in the night-time, finding myself becoming consumed by all these worries.

Yes, eaten up by all these thoughts of strange policemen you had never before seen in your life in the town, arriving from

Warwickshire in the dead of night, with their long grey coats and pulled-down snap-brim hats – braking at the door in a great shiny Wolseley saloon, falling out onto the street without uttering a word & then banging the knocker and bawling away as they stood there at the door:

–Is this the residence of the Irish stamp-thieves, do you mind me asking? Is this the home of a certain confidence trickster, eh?

The exact same as you used to see in the picture-house, all these black-and-white one-reelers filled with alleyways and people running away, & always presented by Edgar Wallace.

Yes, that, I'm afraid, was exactly what it was like in our lane now, with the neighbours trepidatiously beginning to arrive, still clad in their nightclothes – blinking anxiously under the streetlight and shivering coldly as if to say: 'Ah yes, so here we are once more – with them up to the very same old carry-on as before.'

I wonder will they ever learn, you'd hear them say.

Meaning: that crowd, of course.

But with it all turning out to be a lot of old phooey.

Just my imagination taking a hike & running away.

I still can't believe that I did it, though – mislaid the book of approvals, gone and made such a fool of myself.

Knowing how important it was to take care of them.

–I must have left them in the chicken house, I said.

Being almost one hundred per cent certain as I made my way once more down the street towards the square, and then back up by the barber's towards the henhouse.

Repeating to myself as I nervously chipped some stones with my toe: very soon, it will all be over.

& the approvals book will once more be back where it belongs, tucked safely inside the pocket of my corduroy shorts.

No go, I'm afraid.

Even though I spent three hours there, turning the whole place up & down.

No, not so much as a single thing did I find, getting myself all worked up as I started into it all over again, examining this and triple-checking that, standing there under the sloped wooden rafters, in the dry dead air & dust that would choke you – with no end of poor old raggedy broiler hens gazing out pitifully, hopelessly overcrowded in their pens, burbling and pleading among the woodchips please can you help us please please please.

& which I'd gladly have done, that is if I'd been in any position to do so, & hadn't been equally overcome by the very self-same anxiety myself.

As I hoped against hope for a glimpse of either Queen Victoria or George, as a matter of fact even the stupidest old stamp from any dumb old country at all.

I hoped & hoped, but in the end – still nothing.

The following morning I woke up in a state.

Thinking to myself: don't worry, it'll be fine.

Before hearing the letterbox in the hallway going: thlupp!

& landing there on the lino, a cream vellum envelope which, when open, revealed the following: EXTREMELY IMPORTANT. DO NOT IGNORE!

With all these warnings inside when I opened it about 'liability' and – underlined in red – extreme penalties now pending.

I somehow succeeded in persuading myself it was a joke – with absolutely nothing to worry about at all.

Until, at least, another arrived exactly one week later. With even more electric red warnings stamped inside.

I couldn't believe it when I heard the heavy breathing behind me.

–What's this? I hear my father inquiring.

With my mother appearing, almost as if by magic.

–A bill, she answered. it's definitely nothing to worry about, though. Because I'll pay it, Benny. I've money put aside.

–Money put aside? Bill? he said, what on earth are you talking about? I'm not expecting any bill.

–I couldn't really say, I heard my mother reply, however, I expect it's probably the gas. Give it here, I'll go up now this very minute and I'll arrange to pay it.

She smoothed her hands on her apron and nodded decisively.

–Ah now, bills, and laughed, they are one thing you can always be sure of.

& then went back inside to do the dishes – you could hear her humming away her favourite song, 'Whatever Will Be Will Be' and then stopping in the middle to hear what it was my father was saying.

–This isn't a bill, he said as he glared at me, it isn't a bill & you know it. What is it?

I said nothing – because I didn't know what.

To say, I mean.

–Are you listening? I heard my father demand again, are you deaf? Didn't you hear?

Then he just grunted and pushed his way past me, slamming the front door loudly behind him. And that was the end of it, I'm happy to be able to say.

***

At least until sometime after midnight when I heard his footsteps ascending the stairs, & gradually looked up to see him standing in the bedroom doorway.

Straight away, you could tell he'd been drinking.

–Look at this, he said as he approached.

It was a rhino in the jungle, standing by a muddy lake.

In the middle of a great big multicoloured diamond, with directly underneath him, the elegantly scripted lettering – the company name:

Bridgnorth Stamp Co., Warwickshire.

It was probably one of the nicest stamps I've ever seen – all the way from Tanganyika, it transpired.

–Hmph? he said, his plump cheeks flushed. And: hmph? again, tapping the purple-covered booklet with the tip of his finger.

–So what have you got to say about this?

I said I didn't know.

–I'm sorry, he said, but I need an explanation – so please can you give me one? Any kind of a one will do.

But I couldn't think of any.

Which was why he began to shred the letter.

–They can do what they like. I won't pay it, he said.

Then he began to work on the envelope until it was more or less unrecognisable.

–I won't, do you see. Are you listening to me?

Then he moved back a bit & stumbled against the piss-bucket, a sweat breaking out on his forehead as he stood there gazing out the window.

–I know what I'd give them, the likes of Winston Churchill. Who do they think they are?

I didn't know who he meant by Winston Churchill.

Or what he had to do with anything.

As I lay there clutching the top of the blanket and tried the best I could to think of something to say – anything!

–I'll show them, he said, with his clenched fists opening and closing, think I have nothing better to do than fork out hard-earned money for stamps that I never ordered? Because, as far as I'm concerned, Bridgnorth and all of Warwickshire, yes and

Churchill & all the rest of them – they can all go and have a royal good fuck to themselves, that's what they can do!

As over he comes and takes me by the hand, not holding it tight or anything – with it lying limply on the edge of the bed as he sits there, looking down at all the devastated fragments of envelope on the floor, manipulating them with the point of his toe.

Before turning around to look at me and smile – but so vague & distant that it made me feel frightened.

Not because he was going to hit me or anything – it was something even deeper than that.

–Don't you worry your head about them, he said, for as far as anyone in this family is concerned, all of England and the First Lord of the Admiralty – they can all go to hell, so far as I'm concerned.

–I know! I suddenly heard myself exclaim aloud.

Even though I didn't – didn't know anything at all in fact.

& most of all, why I had said it.

Why I had even opened my mouth.

–Are you going to do something about it? he asked.

And which, for some stupid reason, had the effect of making me want to laugh out loud.

–Yes yes, I will! I shrieked.

But when I looked again, my father was gone – with the piss-lake from the bucket slowly & steadily spreading its tentacles out across the floor, with little bits of paper still floating on the top, just like the boats we used to make when it rained.

So that, I suppose, was what you might call 'philately'.

Yes, that, I'm afraid, was the approvals.

Chapter 3

The Two Blanchflowers

I couldn't honestly say, not right down to the last, how many patients exactly have taken their leave and been relocated out to Portrane – but it would have to be well into double figures. Leaving the old stalwarts, as Dr Cecil likes to call us, here to look after the fort.

–You're quite a collection of characters, he says, as Betty Spaghetti goes rushing past twirling a bit of paper – yes, sterling individuals.

With the most 'sterling' of them all, at least in my humble opinion, being the aforementioned Ricky The Shabs – at least when it comes to the 'character' stakes.

Did you know that whenever he came in here first that they used to have to lead him around on a reins?

Well, they did.

&, before you start saying oh that's terrible and threatening to ring up the radio to complain, if you'd seen him back then, I can tell you you'd know why.

But he's OK now – at least if you don't cross him.

Because I'm sorry to have to tell you that he burnt his father and mother to death in their council house in Drimnagh & has been confined here since while they go through the legal paper-work and assess his general mental state.

What keeps him going is this idea that he's going to be discovered, not as innocent or anything, like you might see in the
movies – I mean in the film and theatre business.

Every day he comes in he's a hundred per cent certain that
today is going to be the day.

It's only just a matter of time, bro' Frank, he insists.

And then off he goes, laughing, with his hands in his pockets
& his baseball cap turned around arseways, as usual.

I made a bad mistake with him one day – saying he reminded
me of a fellow I knew that had the 'jaundies' – meaning your face
turned all yellow, like it sometimes does in the later stages of cancer.

–O, man, you is so fucking racist! he says, saying that. That is
way so fucking bad, bro'!

As he tried to hit me a wallop hissing through his two front
teeth.

After that, then, he started into me this big long lecture.

–Because what you got to understand, Old School, is that at
the end of the day what you are is just an old-time Irish potato
man and you don't know nutting. Because you know what The
Ricks is? Bro, he is Chinese – and you had better not forget that,
Old School. Or I is going to take you down. Big time!

He never so much as listens to a word you're saying, his ears
bunged up with the buds of his phone, skidding along in a baggy-
fit purple shell suit, shaking his flat-top.

I did my best to make it up between us by finding this terrific
duster coat on eBay.

Man, I have to say, he went completely wild!

–Jackie Chan, he says, aiming these wild kicks.

He has taken this past while to making action movies on
his phone.

& is always telling me about them & their different plots, but
to be honest I rarely pay much heed.

Being way too busy thinking about the old times, including various aspects of Winston Churchill et al. – along with, believe it or not, exotic flora & fauna & fruit of good old Tanganyika, I'm sorry to have to say.

And remembering the gnawing anxiety that I'd experienced for the rest of that night as I lay there thinking about the approvals after Da had gone – becoming more and more convinced that I could hear the screeching tyres and the clanging bell of the Wolseley pulling up outside.

As all the neighbours began appearing once again.

It's funny the things that you think when you're worried, sedatives or no sedatives. But then I've always been like that – and now was no different.

As I took up my position on the old wooden bench underneath the spreading leaves of the linden, where all the names of former patients & the bits of things that they had to say are crudely carved in deep in the bark.

I knew them all, & their voices tend to come & go.

–Frank, my man, you sure did go and screw it up back then.

I didn't realise I was perspiring heavily – as I often did when too many queued up at once. Thoughts, I mean.

–Yes, that would be correct, I heard someone else suggest, no matter how he protests, because if he hadn't gone and been so careless in the first instance, none of what happened later might ever even have taken place.

–That's right, I heard another wholeheartedly agree, because it was up to him to look after the booklet & if he hadn't been so inattentive, then maybe his poor father, God love him, would never have gotten into such a dreadful state.

You could sit there arguing all day with these viewpoints, putting your case & pointing out this and that – but it never worked. They never seemed to listen.

But that didn't stop me.

–Excuse me, I said, I'm sorry, but would you mind holding it right there?

–What's that? they said.

I tore at a hunk of grass & continued.

–All I'm doing is trying to explain, I said, attempting to give you the objective facts of the case – that's all.

–Oh, is that what you're doing? Very well then, go ahead.

So I did.

Explaining at length how I'd scoured the length & breadth of the chicken house, to no avail.

–I spent a whole day searching, I said.

–A whole day?

–Yes, I continued, so it wasn't like you could say I didn't care. It wasn't like I was being careless. It was just unfortunate. It was just an accident. These things happen.

–What a pity, they said, all that effort …

–With the booklet of approvals never to be seen again.

–It was tragic, really. Considering what was to happen between him and his father.

So, as I'm sure you can imagine, after thinking all that – I wasn't feeling exactly *Top of the Pops*.

But who did I go and run into then only old Mrs Beacon, and that cheered me up immensely. She's been here for years, like myself, and is more or less in charge of the cleaning. Although whether that's official or not, I don't know, and I'm not sure if anyone else around here is either.

I was playing push-penny when up she comes behind me.

–Ah yes, London, she says, in this sad regretful long-ago voice.

Which I have to say I enjoy whenever I hear it.

She was working in London during the war, do you see.

& says that Ireland is only a dump.

—Not like there, she says. There was nothing I used to like better than popping over to Lyons' Corner House on The Strand – and having myself a cuppa & a nice little halfpenny bun.

The more she talks the more English she becomes.

—I was never happier than when I was there, she goes on, with all the pals I had, not to mention any number of gentleman admirers – whether or not you believe that, Frank.

Then she told me that she knew Benny Hill. The comedian, that is.

—He asked me out, as a matter of fact, she says, & if you don't take offence I would have to say that you remind me a little of him. Because you really are an amusing chap, Frank – at least whenever one finds you amenable. & so in his way was Bernard, as I called him. Lord, when I think of it, those dancing eyes and that little impish smile. *It's That Man Again* – that was the revue he brought me to. A natural he was, a real clown that old Benny: so similar to you, in many ways, Frank – with the very same cocky attitude.

And who still turns up all the time on telly – on UK Gold, a special favourite of mine. As a matter of fact he was on only this morning – directly after *TOTP*, with Jimmy Savile: Ee-urgh! Ee-urgh!

Enough said about him.

Give me the keys of the hospital, if you please.

Very well, Mr Savile – there you are.

I had arranged to meet The Professor in the arboretum & he was all ears when he heard about my latest plans for *The Big Yaroo* – as I rabbited away to beat the band – with no end of facts and figures at my disposal, having made sure to enter them all in my notebook.

Before beginning to realise that my companion hadn't been listening to a word I said – specifically regarding an article I'd been preparing for my sports column on the life of the famous footballer Danny Blanchflower, the Northern Irish international centre forward from the year 1963.

& which I soon realised, I can tell you, when I look over and what is The Professor doing only kneeling down as he scrabbles away in some earth, shaking his head and talking to himself.

Then he comes back and hands me a worm.

But if you think he wasn't listening to a word you were saying – as so often happens, that is where you are absolutely and one hundred percent wrong.

Because do you know what he turns around and goes and says then?

–But what about his brother Jackie?

With it transpiring that, after all my preparation and purported wealth of knowledge, I hadn't known half of what The Professor had to say.

–Yes, Mr Frank, you may very well feel assured of your facts. But on this occasion, I feel I am faced with no choice but to disabuse you of certain assumptions you appear to be making – because, in actual fact there were *two* sporting stars in the illustrious Blanchflower sporting dynasty.

Then, what's he do?

Gets up and walks away, leaving me there looking down at the blackhead.

Which is what we used to call them in the old times.

Worms, I mean.

Just squirming there and looking up as if to say:

–I mean, what the fuck?

But I really do like him – Professor Big Brains.

Although – so often, I suppose like myself – he appears to be in some kind of mental torment, but remains afraid to acquaint you of its character.

However, torment or not, I knew that as usual, he'd be right concerning his 'amazing sporting facts' – and just as soon as I made my way back to my office, I ran a comprehensive check on Wikipedia.

With, to my astonishment, it turning out that the famous association footballing family had once been embroiled in a minor sporting scandal – when the aforementioned Danny had stormed off the set of *This Is Your Life* in a fury.

Which was a popular television programme from the sixties, loved by everyone – but by none more so than my parents – my mother especially, most likely because it had been presented by an Irishman.

But not only that – one who wore a neatly pressed dinner jacket and dicky bow and didn't smell of whiskey and Guinness, being likely to lose his temper and smash up the whole TV studio.

My mother, in particular, was very fond of Eamonn Andrews, and I remember her telling me once that if she hadn't accepted my father's proposal that, likely as not, Eamonn would have been the man.

& which makes me laugh, even to this day – thinking about Da in his regimental blazer flying across to London in a private jet.

& arriving back home every weekend, swinging his briefcase – filled with Lucky Lumps for me to eat.

Now that would have been the 'good old 1960s!' for sure, if it could have happened, I thought to myself as I turned the knob on the transistor as high as it could possibly go, and then rolled up my sleeves as I set about my work – being as pleased as Punch when I heard Sandie Shaw, of whom I am the world's number one top fan, chanting her heart out as she told all the world about her adventures in Paris. To which she had nipped over, just for the day, and happened to encounter a certain dashing – and really quite forward – gentleman, or so it would appear.

–*M'sieu Dupont*! sings Sandie, *I know it's wrong!*

& to which I reply:

–Oh no, Sandie, it's not. You go right ahead there, girl!

With the rain pouring down in my mind as she flies outta town and arrives at a pavement cafe with old Dupont, and I polish the living blue fuck out of my racer.

Then, as soon as I am finished, stand up and give the salute, like I'm at any moment ready to start spouting the French national anthem.

–Beat that, Dupont! I say, as off goes my oily old rag behind the bins.

& away I go back up towards the refectory – on the scent of the 'Cookstown sizzle', as me and The Prof call sausages.

Or bangers.

Chapter 4

The Island of Cuba

The Big Chief Yaroo Kid – that, perhaps, might be a good name to put on me at this stage, now that all the former residents of Fizzbag hospital have finally packed their cases and headed off out to North County Dublin, that old happy end-of-days resort by the ocean – presumably filling their faces with no end of candyfloss and periwinkles and enjoying plenty of bracing rambles along the promenade.

With the result that, apart from the few others I've mentioned already, and who most of the time remain inside their rooms, thanks to Dr Cecil I pretty much exclusively have the run of the whole place.

And, in return for some light caretaking duties – which primarily involve raking leaves and picking up papers – I am permitted to wander wherever I may please. And which is why, if you happen to drop by, you'll see that old Frank twirling his pointed stick with aplomb as yet another sweet wrapper goes pitchaow! into the bottom of the basket.

That is, of course, when the gentleman concerned is not keeping himself busy down in the environs of the pump house polishing up his trusty old bicycle – a sturdy machine, which was left behind by Mr 'Blenners' Blennerhassett, God be good to him, whenever he finally passed away.

He was always heading off around Ireland on bikes – 'being a keen naturalist', as he used to say.

There was nothing old Blenners didn't know about birds and flowers. Himself and Muggsy Big Brains, they used to always enjoy these great chats in the arboretum about every conceivable subject under the sun.

But now, like so many, he's departed from this earth, and all that remains of his mortal presence is his bicycle – or 'Madame La Road Runner', as I like to call her. Meep! Meep!

Although I'm sure there's machines that could go a lot faster – but, all the same, she's still in very good shape, and will be more than capable of completing the task I have in mind – my own personal version, I guess, of the Tour de France.

La Madame is light aluminium and has a wire basket and a saddle, not to mention twelve top-speed gears. All – thanks to my assiduous efforts over the past six months or so – I am happy to say, in perfect working order, perfected whenever Dr Cecil or his associate, the hospital pastor Fr McGivney, are not around – because the pair of them, believe me, would go stark raving bonkers if they happened to catch me.

Mr Blennerhassett died back in 2007 or maybe 2008 – so it's been lying there since with nobody bothering their arses about it, including myself, at least until recently.

I can remember his auntie coming for his effects and seeing her standing in the chapel corridor, looking out. Looking out at what, you may ask – well, the rain, what else?

With this awful look of sadness flickering past in her eyes – the exact very same as you'll see with Professor Big Brains, always on the verge of breaking down, or so it seems.

As along comes Dr Cecil to cheer him up.

–Ah yes, he was a great old man for the birds, he says.

–Aye, says The Professor, Mr Blennerhassett, he sure did love them birdies & no mistake.

He gave out to me once for trying to escape. Something, which, I'm sorry to have to say, I find myself deeply embarrassed about now.

Mainly because I made such a botch job of it.

Something, which, I can guarantee you this time, isn't going to happen. Although a lot of my catastrophic failure the first time around I have no hesitation in putting down to my medication at the time.

& with my new-found confidence probably being attributable to the feeling that I've got an awful lot more space to enjoy these days.

With plenty of room to breathe, you know?

Without people coming up and enquiring into your business – pestering you with all these stupid little queries about this and that, until in the end you often find you can take it no more, and then just turn around & say:

–Shut the fuck up!

In a way, walking around, it's like being handed the deeds of your own private little country – one with a stamp displaying your own head as king.

So, all in all, they're good times – yes, I would have to say so.

As up I get every morning, with nothing on my mind except getting out there and polishing that old Road Runner after breakfast.

One of the spots where I like to keep her parked whenever that old Fr Ron isn't around is up against the railings surrounding my old friend The Mother of God.

& who, God bless her, is still standing there right where she was that very first day when I came strolling through the gates – only I am sorry to have to be honest and say that in so many ways she appears to be in very poor shape indeed.

Not that that's particularly surprising, seeing as some of the patients – I have their names! – used to sometimes go to the toilet behind her & even write stuff about their lives in marker on her back.

Then, of course, there's the inevitable damage caused by constant erosion, with her face having more or less turned green and a great big lump tore out of her shoulder.

Not, to be honest, that The Lady herself seems in any way unduly concerned – just staring straight ahead at the buses going by the hospital, or bits of paper blowing fast on a windy day.

Me & her used to get along real well, but not so much since my uncle died.

It's sad, yes I know, but that's the way it is, I'm afraid.

Why do things like that have to happen?

It was Fr Ron who gave me the news.

–I'd like you to sit down, Frank, if you please, he said.

I think, to be honest, I already knew what was coming.

He had passed away in an old folks' home in Croydon – with nobody, not one.

–No, none of his relatives at his bedside, said the priest.

& which was bad, but don't ask me why I had to go and put the blame on Our Lady.

Because that's what I did.

& then having this dream, tossing & turning about The Scuttler – yes, Corrigan the handyman, coming along with his barrow and whistling without a care – before arriving over and tipping the contents out at my feet.

At first I thought it was a shrivelled-up turnip.

Then, on second inspection, it revealed itself as a human head – that of my dead uncle.

& wearing, of all things, a velvet pillbox hat with a brown short-ish veil.

–God has turned his face away from you, it said with a rasp, so it makes no difference what you do, & whether you decide to pray or not.

Then it had laughed as The Scuttler lifted it up by the dangling roots and tossed it, still whistling, back into the barrow.

As off he went.

And I found myself waking up, lying there stiff as a board.

There was a time when I used to have dreams like that all the time – but not so much now.

Not since Fr Ronnie came around.

Only for him I'd probably still be having them.

It was him came up with the idea of *The Big Yaroo*.

–Something to occupy your mind, he said.

& boy was that old Ronners right about that!

Because he had this facility – this ability, I don't know – of somehow being able to read your mind.

Anyone else would have laughed at me, I know.

–You want to start a what? they'd have said.

Never mind offering to find some way to arrange financial support & assistance – to avail of all these start-up grants that he seemed to know nearly everything about. Because he does seem to have this special ability to persuade other people to give away money – & endowed me with a special allowance for the purpose of purchasing a brand-new desktop computer, with all the software you need pre-loaded.

& which is why I'm going to dedicate the magazine to him, & include a special double-page centre spread on hurling, which he loves.

& which I, I'm afraid, know sweet motherfucking fuck all about, not that he minds.

With my own speciality being the American Funnies insert.

Including a special little story, composed entirely by me, about how the CIA invasion of Cuba affected the small town in which I was born.

& which might be hard for some people to understand now, what with the way news comes and goes so fast – but back then it wasn't like that.

As a matter of fact, for months before it happened, there was nothing else that seemed to be talked about.

–That will put it up to the Russians, I remember hearing Hughie 'Kerensky' Mackleson remarking as a few of us stood at the corner, smoking.

Nikita Khrushchev had been blathering away on the telly that day, all about the rockets they had stacked up in Cuba, ready to tear the hole off New York.

–Just let the fucker try it, Kerensky grunted, because we're well able for him in this town. I see there's a film on in the picture house called *The Russians Are Coming, the Russians Are Coming*. Oh, is that a fact? Well, come on then if you please, Nikita and friends – let's have the lot of you. Because if you want to talk about islands, this little one here called Ireland it would knock seven shades of shite out of you and any Cuba, rockets or no rockets!

Rubbing his hands as he went off into the Tower Bar, giving me a wave, calling back that he'd see me later.

Chapter 5
New York City, 1947

So I was telling you about Big Brains Muggsy, what a guy.

I'm sorry to have to say that he was at it again yesterday not long after I got this urge, don't ask me why – just as soon as I was one hundred per cent certain that the coast was clear – to scoot away on down to the pump house to lay my hands on that tar-burning little beauty The Road Runner & take her out for another run around the block.

And am enjoying myself no end, having devised this elaborate practice circuit for myself around the back of the hospital, churning up the gravel with figure eights and the whole bloody lot.

Hooray, and zoom – no stopping me at all.

When I look up, not thinking – and who do I see standing in front of me? Only The Professor himself with a face on him like thunder.

–Ní hé sin go ceart! he says, and hands me this piece of paper he says is a speeding ticket.

–Just what do you think you're playing at, man? he demands.

–I'm sorry, I replied, I didn't know what I was doing.

And somehow, don't ask me why – that seemed to satisfy him.

As he replaces his little black notebook in his pocket and says:

–It's time to stop all this nonsense, do you hear me now, Frank? So, come along with me now and we'll go and sit for a while in the shade of our old friend the linden. What do you say to that?

–Very good, I says.

& then off we go.

It really is a majestic tree.

I don't know how many names have been dug into it over the years – there's even a date I scratched into it myself, oh, years ago.

Back when I was a cub, as they used to say.

If you look very closely you can just about make it out:

Rem FB, March 14, 1965

We had a great old chat, me & him, just sitting there, about this and that.

But do you know what's distressing? The fact that sometimes, usually completely out of nowhere, he'll find himself afflicted by this sudden awareness – realisation – of just how foolish it sounds, what he has just said.

& whenever that happens, you've never seen such shame.

–It's like someone is acting me out inside my head, manipulating my thoughts in order to make me say the most frightful things.

Only then what does he go and do?

Repeat the whole darned lot all over again, word for word.

He'd been telling me all about this football match – not that I was interested, for as far as I'm concerned, a Gatling gun's not good enough for the half of them.

But anyway, on he went, in the course of his descriptions making all these wild, extravagant gestures – as, with one mighty swing of his boot, he buries the ball in the back of the net!

But that was just the start of it, as he listed off this roll call of stars of yesteryear.

With me nodding away, making sure to keep my beak shut.

Now he was rabbiting on about New York, where the All-Ireland football final had been staged, a once-in-a-lifetime event, in the Polo Grounds in 1947.

And is going great guns till he forgets all about the goals that are being scored & starts talking about how lovely his fiancée was.

& how delicate and refined she had looked in the lobby of the Waldorf Hotel.

—Yes, the Waldorf, he beamed, before fondly reminiscing on their walk that very first afternoon in Central Park, with himself and Colleen Turley from Drung holding hands and laughing as off they went on the trolleybus – & then striding, the pair of them, along Madison Avenue, taking in all the sights as they went.

—Radio City Music Hall, he mused.

As I thumped my paw and, in a big loud American bleat, replied:

—Wow; Professor!

—Yes, Frank, he said, and directly above, guess what?

—The Empire State Building, I suggested.

—Correct and right! beamed the big brains genius and after that, the statue of what?

—Liberty, Prof, Liberty for sure and certain.

—You are right, for certain sure, he said, & away with the pair of us, right up to the very top.

Then he shook his head and stared at the ground.

—Ah yes, he began anew, you don't get the opportunity to meet the likes of her in your life, I'm afraid – much less find yourself fortunate enough to be their employer. Because, you see, I was her direct superior, Frank – in the little country school where we both taught. Like Maureen O'Hara she was – with those long rusty ringlets sweeping down past her shoulders and a scattering of the loveliest freckles on her cheeks. Lord above, what a fool and a useless cretin am I, and that's a fact – for what I done.

Then what did he do, as so many times before.

—I know, Frank. Let's go and hide.

& without saying so much as another word, grabbed hold of me by the arm and dragged me all the way across the lawn, pushing me in behind the linden.

Before stripping his teeth and violently striking the tree trunk repeatedly.

—But then what did Miss Colleen Turley expect, the strap? I mean, did she really think someone in such a responsible position as I – would be willing to spend my life with someone who had behaved little better than a common prostitute? Because if that's what she thought – well, I'm sorry, but I don't think so.

Then he turns around and closes one eye, staring right at me, collecting his thoughts.

—I want you now to tell me the truth. Do you genuinely think that at my age I've got nothing better to do than spread false rumours about people?

—No, I said, no Professor – I absolutely do not.

—I'm glad, he said, because the simple facts of the matter are that there was nobody more than me looking forward to spending time with my lovely fiancée in America.

He shook his head sadly.

—But, as soon became obvious, I needn't have bothered my backside looking forward to anything. Not where Colleen Turley was concerned.

He was now gathering up leaves and arranging them all into a little circular pile.

—When we got to the top, he continued, of the Statue of Liberty, my Colleen said she had never seen me so happy. And why on earth wouldn't I be happy, I replied, when I have the company of the lovely Miss Turley to enjoy here in New York City, and along with that the prospect of our team bringing home the cup.

& now he was back in their luxurious and capacious apartments on the twenty-third floor of the Waldorf Hotel, New York

1947, reading *The New York Times* in his striped pyjamas, laying sprawled on that great king-size bed, puffing away on his pipe.

It was as if the memory proved too much – as he delivered the air a mighty punch.

& squealed there in front of me, leaping two or three feet high in the air.

–And once more the ball is in the back of the net!

& after that then, beginning to weep uncontrollably, something I'd witnessed him doing before – & not once or twice, either.

& which, I suppose, made it clear that that was what was probably in store for me too – now that I was getting older.

With there never being very much chance of a way out – as bits of your mind & your soul began fading.

So that's why I'd like to go out with a bang.

Because I just couldn't face it – ending up like Muggsy, one of the brainiest men I've ever known.

& I know he'd give my escape his blessing – if he could remain himself for long enough.

Instead of walking around a linden tree in circles, acting himself out the way he thinks he used to be.

Wringing his hands as he repeats in the same hoarse voice:

–Cavan 2–11, Kerry 2–7. Cavan 2–11, Kerry 2–7.

I've developed this habit, in recent times, of grinding my teeth – I don't know why.

& I was doing it now.

& kept on doing it until I looked up and realised that he was gone – Professor Big Brains, I mean.

With there not being a sound about the place, only the birds – starlings, mostly.

I'll often get this sense of loss.

Out of nowhere, it comes in waves.

& I'll see my uncle.

& the rest of them.

It seems to come in like the tide – and now, sure enough, here it was again.

All the things we do that we regret.

–Did you know she came to my room in the middle of the night, he had said to me, shaking – and us not married!

Then he said that if word had ever got back to Drung he could have lost his job and been disgraced.

–Why did she have to do it, he wept, but even more importantly – why didn't I welcome her into my bed?

–What was wrong with us in those days? he says, I'm all confused.

–That's why I'm looking forward to not being here any more, he says, knocking his brow like a woodpecker against the tree, do you know what I'm trying to say when I tell you that?

–Yes, I replied, and I wasn't telling lies.

Because I really do know exactly what he means.

Seeing as, for some time, I've been thinking along those lines myself.

With the only difference being that this time my departure is going to be an absolute cracker.

Chapter 6
Mysterious People

I've never seen anything like the changes these days, have you?

Because I don't suppose you know it, but back in the little town where I was born there was only four phones altogether, one belonging to the doctor, then the priest and after that a couple of others I don't know who they were, the police I suppose.

Well, one thing for sure is – you can forget about all that now.

Because soon you'll have the phone surgically inserted underneath your skin – or so I was reading just this morning in the library.

Not that I'm complaining – I'm all for it.

It's just that the future – it's not what you expected.

With no flying cars, like they promised, or jetpacks.

But any amount of smartphones, Wi-Fi cams, high-definition TVs and all the rest of it.

The Professor is convinced it's going to end bad.

–We are living in times unprecedented in history, he says. Bombarded as we are by a veritable blitz of information data and noise, in this accursed digital Babel of non-stop chaos, burdened beneath the crushing weight of immediate and proximate stimuli! How could we have ever have anticipated such a degree of absolute, entirely unregulated mayhem?

–Yes, I replied, I suppose there you are.

Whatever that was supposed to mean.

But, after all, what are you meant to say?

When all you've ever been expecting, as I say, is the jetpacks and the so-called robot butlers & all the rest of it.

& then, when it comes – the future – it doesn't look a bit like what you've been promised.

I was talking about it yesterday with Mrs Beacon in the office, which she insists on coming in to clean every day, without fail.

–Oh, I pass no heed, she says, and goes on sweeping, let them do what they like, as far as I'm concerned. For they'll do that anyway.

Then she says:

–Would you get out of my way, there's another bit of dirt there under your feet – & let me tell you this, if you're going to make this magazine business of yours a success, then you had better smarten up when it comes to improving the way things look. It's not just enough to stick up a few pictures – a proper editorial office must have style. A bit of class, you know?

–Right you be, Mrs Beacon, I says.

Because, although I know she can be cranky by times, there isn't one in this hospital who can beat her – not so far as I'm concerned anyway.

& which is why I let her in on my secret.

Which I'll tell you about later on.

& I'm glad I did, because Mrs Beacon is someone – someone you know you can trust.

& I know that now for sure.

So I'm glad I took her into my confidence.

A problem shared is a problem halved – that's what she always says herself.

Whenever I got the first symptoms in my gut, it was her who drove me into the hospital – because Fr Ron wasn't able to do it.

Yes, all the way out to the James Connolly Memorial Hospital in Blanch.

We had a great old journey that day, with me being so excited I just can't tell you – seeing as I hadn't been out of the place in years.

Taking in the names of all these shops – Costcutter, Penneys, Vodafone, EuroGiant.

&, because they were so new, & colourful along with it – that's maybe why I went just a little over the top.

& why the doctor had asked me to try and please calm down.

They had put me in a wheelchair, I remember, for a whole morning – and I thought this was the best of crack, not realising at the time just how serious it might become.

& which, of course, it did.

–I'm not ready to be Ironside yet, Doc, I said.

But, as I can see now, he hadn't a clue what I was talking about.

Because nobody knows about Ironside now – or any of those old-style 1960s detectives.

Mary gave me her prayer book that day – just leaned over and slipped it into my lap.

–I don't bother with missals or prayer books any more, I told her.

& was sorry, in a way, that I'd opened my mouth.

Because she'd looked kind of hurt.

But it's true, though.

Because whenever you read them all they'll do is tell you that all your old friends and relatives – you don't have to worry because none of them are really ever truly gone. And that they're all just up there waiting, all sitting around a table in what they call the communion of saints. And it's a very nice thing to believe – yes, but of course it is. With the only thing being that, unfortunately, it isn't true.

Because every one of them is gone – aren't they?

And the only person waiting above the clouds is Mr Nobody – with or without fucking wings.

See if I care.

With the real reason why I know about that being that, up until the night they brought the news to my room about my uncle – I suppose up till then I'd been nurturing a small bit of hope.

Not a lot maybe – just enough so as not to give up altogether.

But then the knock came:

–I wonder could I have a word?

So that was the end of the missals after that.

–I'm sorry to say that it's progressive, stage three, I remember the consultant saying, tearing a page off a notepad and handing it to Mary.

Don't ask me what was on it, I forget.

More cancer bullshit, spores tearing loose – on the rampage.

Who cares, I said – and, to be honest, at the time I didn't.

But I suppose that that's what it's like when you're young – and after all, I had only turned sixty, hadn't I, ha ha.

Woah, boys.

It'll be teatime soon.

Was I telling you about my appetite recently?

Somehow, it seems, I can't stop eating.

Must be to do with anxiety & anticipating – because I really am excited about what's in store over the next few days.

Mrs B's noticed how much weight I've put on.

But I'm so agitated I just can't stop horsing it into me – especially when it comes to sausages.

She says I'm worse than Desperate Dan.

& started laughing her head off when she saw the bit I'd written about Exhibit X, which had just rolled off the printer as soon as she'd finished her cleaning.

—I wouldn't fancy running into that, she says, would that be to do with the aliens, I wonder?

—That remains to be seen, Mrs B, I said, I haven't quite yet finished working it out.

—You're an awful character, you and this *Big Yaroo* of yours, she says.

But making sure to add that she'll definitely buy a copy.

—Or two, she says, heaving the Hoover out the door.

& leaving me there to beaver away at my computer.

& I have to say, even though she complains, that so far as I'm concerned, the office is coming along great all the time.

With a great big notice right up there above my head, on the wall:

NO SMOKING!
By Order – FB.

Not that it seems to bother Ron – who was in here again this afternoon, puffing away like there was no tomorrow – strange carry-on for a priest, you'd have to say, at least one who is supposedly in charge of the place.

In spite of his weakness for never shutting his fucking mouth about that stupid game of hurling, so far as I'm concerned, the best thing about that old Fr Ron McGivney is the assistance he gave me whenever it finally came to selecting the most appropriate name for the magazine.

Because I really had my brains racked trying to think.

—*Frank's Funnies*, I said, what about that?

—Ah for the love of God, he said, can you not try and do a bit better than that?

Boys' Own Paper was another name I'd suggested – but it didn't take him long to demolish that one too.

–Look, here, Frank, I remember him saying one day out of the blue, leaning across as he made this sketch on his knee – laughing away as he was doing it, before handing me over a picture of myself, with this huge big bubble inflating out of my mouth. 'Yaroo', it said.

Have you ever heard of the light-bulb moment?

Well, that was it – we had our name.

All thanks to the famous Ron McGivney.

And if you think that the clergyman's work was completed after that, then you don't know just how wrong you actually are.

Because that, in fact, was just the beginning.

With him not only making them give me the money but helping me to decorate the whole place and put down lino – and turning an ordinary old wooden garden shed into a state-of-the-art publisher's office.

–*Voilà!* he declared.

Man, what a character.

& it really was looking good.

But the best thing of all that I got was the tiger rug on eBay.

Guess how much?

Only eighteen yo-yos.

Smashing price, I have to say.

Then I varnished the place myself, from top to bottom.

& sat down at my desk, tugging down my luminous green eyeshade (a mere two yo-yos, believe it or not) and began hammering away at the keyboard for all I was worth.

It must have been near nine o' clock when I finished.

As *chug-chug whirr*! went the Canon and out rolled my latest:

Mysterious People

(A *Big Yaroo* tale for winter nights)

'Slow down here,' thought Fudsy Buddly to himself as his car rumbled over the bumpy country road. 'A nice quiet holiday in a nice quiet Irish village,' he said to himself.

He was really looking forward to a few days' holiday with his friend. It would take his mind off his hands. He gripped the steering wheel with the lightest possible touch. He knew that the slightest pressure from his black-gloved hands would buckle and crush the wheel.

This amazing strength was part of an accident involving radioactive waste material. Buddly had worked in a scientific institute. There had been an accident. To save valuable equipment and a fellow worker's life he had dragged away a container of radioactive waste. He'd sealed it in a safety room and staggered out.

He woke in hospital to find his hands horribly mutilated. It was thought that he could never use them again. But when he left hospital, he found that his hands had acquired a fantastic strength. For the next few weeks he had to learn to control that strength. At first the things he tried to hold all crumbled. Finally, he managed to control this. But as his hands were still horribly scarred, he always wore skin-tight black gloves.

He regained consciousness inside a glass case. There was equipment outside all around

43

the case. Grey creatures worked at the
machines. One grey creature, larger than
the other, was walking towards the case. It
stopped outside. Slowly the creature pushed
in. A hidden door opened and it stepped in.
Buddly cowered away in fear.

'What do you want?' he asked.

'I am the leader of the people you see
before you. We are the people of the Polidons
— and very soon we will be your masters!'

As Buddly stabbed the air with a limb
that was not a limb — if it ever had been!
With what had once been its hand — if it,
too, had ever been! — fused horribly at the
end — culminating in a sickeningly, vile
disfigurement in an algae-shaded fusion of
obscenely affronted flesh.

Who was this interloper? Who could they be
— all these mysterious people — just exactly
where had they come from?

So, there you are — it's nine to five & at weekends around the
clock, ensuring that I meet my deadline, when I look up and see,
who do you think, only that nosey bastard Corrigan who's always
skulking around — raging, probably, because he can't read. Never
mind edit a magazine.

But I decide to ignore him and going back into writing
my next episode of Exhibit X when I hear a twig crunching
the very same as before — and, sure enough, there he is, with
his great big fucking sickle-shaped head looking in through
the window.

—Don't think I don't know, he starts growling in that sickening auld sour fucking way that he does, oh you can be sure that The Scuttler knows all right. Oh there's not much, you'll find, The Scuttler doesn't know.

—Like who gives a fuck, I says, and go back to my work, as if anyone around here cares about anything you know. Now, go ahead and clear off – I'm busy!

—Shut your impudent effing mouth, you twister! he says then, because I know what you're up to in there – & any chance he gets, The Scuttler'll shop you!

—Oh don't worry, Mr Corrigan, I says, you needn't think I'm not aware of that!

—Yes, you see, because I have the information. So, are you going to tell me what you were doing with the bucket?

I went a bit pale when I heard him saying that, but did the best I could not to let him see.

—Like I care about buckets, I said, would you g'wan to hell out of that, for God's sake, Corrigan, and not be making a damned fool of yourself!

—The way I see it is, he began, you can pretend all you like that this shed is an office, but while you're in this hospital the rules are the same for you as everyone else. And when I was coming past here at seven o'clock this morning, I know I smelt smoke. & it wasn't just ordinary papers you left behind you in the bucket, Oh no, no Sir.

—Not ordinary papers? I heard myself stammer – and you could see that he knew he had me now.

—Don't go acting the innocent with me, he says, & if I were you, I'd be extremely careful. I would take pains to be extremely careful. Yes, to be very careful indeed, I have to say. Because you could find yourself in a whole lot of very hot water.

Then he looked at me queerly and I have to say that I didn't like it.

–That's all I'll say, he repeated, because I've said enough, & I can tell by your face you know what I mean.

–I wouldn't advise you to be saying things like that, I told him.

–I'll say what I like, he shot back and was gone.

And, straight away, I was over in the corner, rolling back the lino and lifting up the loose floorboard where I'd stashed my stack of publications from England. I could have sworn that they'd be gone – but they weren't.

Then I took them away and threw them over the fence. I was still all covered in sweat, but now that I'd dumped them knew that I was fine.

&, after a while, was back to myself as good as new.

It actually felt like a whole new world.

One where that stoop-shouldered meddler The Scuttler Corrigan didn't exist – or, even better, had recently been flattened by a double-decker bus.

It was a great old feeling.

As back I went to my labours – this time p. 2 and the popular feature: 'What Would You Do?' If you happened to find yourself in a situation where three jet fighters were flashing through the sky at 550 mph and suddenly, without warning, one of the pilots had trouble with his oxygen and slumps unconscious as his comrades look on helplessly?

With the answer provided on p. 22.

Next week: 'The Editor Battles the Incas'.

Probably one of the most important features, thanks in the main to Jack Palance, is that old stalwart and all-time favourite, *Believe It or Not*.

Fr Ron especially likes that one.

He says there was a fellow in the seminary seen The Sasquatch.

–Yes, in Maynooth. One Christmas when he stayed over. Out there in the woods, watching everything – not moving a muscle. Scared the life out of him, so it did.

But sometimes you're not sure with that old Fr Ron McGivney.

Whether or not he might be acting the bollocks.

Well, I swear to God, is that the time?

Grub up!

& look – there's Shabs, above on the terrace staring at his watch.

Waving as if to say: come on, Frank, to hell!

Because, of course, it's Thursday, which means my favourite!

Man, but I love that old Chicken Maryland – and after that, a choice of four desserts.

What more could you want after a hard day's editing – in spite of having been given a pain in the nut by Corrigan.

Because that Scuttler, he really does know how to wriggle right under your skin – and just stand there looking at you.

I hate the way he does that.

As if he genuinely does know everything.

That's going on, I mean.

Which is why I have to be very, very careful – not to so much as breathe a word about my plan.

Because it would break my heart if the whole thing went wrong again, like before.

Deep in my heart, I know, though, that it won't.

Because I'm way too cute to be outfoxed by the likes of him.

As off I go and catch up with The Shabs.

Hey, my man, he says, and we go inside – with him blathering away nineteen to the dozen about this film he's just downloaded. *The Rocketeer*, it's called.

& which reminds me when he's talking about it of one me and Joe had invented ourselves this day when we seen Mr Nugent with Winston Irwin the solicitor, crossing the Diamond.

–I never would have dreamed it, I remembered Joe saying, I would never in a million years have suspected.

That he was one of The Umbrella Men, he meant.

–What you on about? says Ricky, rolling his eyes as he gave me this look.

–You'd never, in your wildest dreams, believe that they belonged to a secret international bureau, I said, Mr Nugent & Winston.

–A what? says this other fellow at the bottom of the refectory table, a secret international what?

–Who used, I explained, these motorised, jet-propelled umbrellas to fly and commit robberies. They dressed in business suits and wore bowler hats.

–I had a brother went like you, says your man, & goes on eating.

–Yeah! says The Ricks, that is maybe a good story – only problem is we ain't never gonna see it! Not like *The Rocketeer*, know what I'm saying?

Then turns around and hits me this wallop on the shoulder.

He just doesn't know his own strength, that man.

Chapter 7

Big Day in Annagreevy

Probably the greatest thing of all about the magazine is that I'm going to have it out just in time for the holiday, and if there is one thing I love more than anything in the world as regards comics, it was always that good old Easter Special.

& which I've always had a soft spot for, mostly because of that special and unusual year when my mother got up and looked out of the window and says to me, Frank do you know what I'm going to tell you & I know you won't believe me but it's coming up to Easter Sunday and, honest to God if it isn't coming down out of the heavens.

–Snow! she says, would you credit it, at this time of the year.

But like I said to my mother on that most welcome and auspicious occasion, I didn't care what time it came – just so long as I could look out and see it blanketing the whole country all about us, from the tip of the top of the church steeple to the thistled slopes of the old fort field.

–That was good enough for me, I said. Absolutely sure thing Ma, and she smiled & says to me then:

–Get on your coat!

& away with the pair of us, off out to the Annagreevy river, all covered in lily pads and overhanging laburnum tree branches – to have ourselves a private picnic in the snow.

Believe it or not!

Except that we wouldn't – at least not right now.

Because the temperature had dropped to almost sub-zero levels – so that would mean that our walk would have to be short.

Or, at least we thought so – until, as always seemed to be happening in the town back in them days, who should we happen to meet only Wee Pat Casey – coming stomping with his staff across the rows of hard, starched drills.

–Ah hello there, Mrs! Wee Pat shouts cheerily, already making his way across the field.

Apart from His Majesty Big Brains The Professor, and one or two others, I would have to say that he was one of the nicest men I ever met.

As over he comes, barrelling, in his big long coat and crunching hobnailed boots – debating the value of this recent fall of snow.

–I'm all for it! I heard myself say, it's nearly as good as the one that was in *The Dandy*, Mr Casey!

–He's fond of the reading, Wee Pat, I heard my mother say, anytime I come on him he always seems to have his nose stuck in a comic.

–Ah, boys, the comics! enthused Wee Pat, I used to always love them myself as a nipper – aye, Korky the Cat and what-you-call-him, Mickey Mouse. So, go on there, me young chap, away out of it with you there and do me a favour, make an old-timer happy. Read a scatter of them words in the book for us!

–Go on, said my mother, there's a good lad.

As off I went, a bit shy but still proud.

Clearing my throat as I launched with vigour into the story of Funny Bunny Cuddles – the amusing rabbit from the panels of *Playhour* who loved shoving long spoons into jars.

–Cuddlers Buddlers, all he ever thinks about is jam, I went on. But all the cook could find in the whole of the ship was the tiniest little jar of strawberry. 'Will this do, Sir?' the captain said. 'Do?' gasped Bunny. 'Why that won't last for even two moments. Because I eat jam for every meal and snack!'

–He loves the strawberry, your man, so he does! beamed Wee Pat Casey, nothing will do him till he gets his hands on a pot – & if he hasn't gone and got it plastered all over his face!

And, sure enough, when I moved on to the very next panel, I saw that indeed he had – lying there covered in great big chunky pink lumps, looking swivel-eyed and sick with the spoon.

As my mother began singing, ever so softly:

Easter bunny
Looking funny
With his basket of eggs
Bells are ringing
Children singing,
'Hooray for Easter Day!'

& which is why, I suppose, I've kind of adopted it as a sort of anthem, kind of cheering me on as I get everything ready for this coming weekend.

Which will really see me making my mark on the world, something I've never ever done before – at least not in the way that a decent person ought to.

But all that is now set to change – & with all of it recorded, for posterity, in *The Big Yaroo*.

Which I think of more as a celebration than anything – & if it's a way of saying goodbye, it's also a kind of memorial to the lovely days that the two of us had together.

My mother & I, and all my other old friends in the town.

Way back.

So that's why I want to get it all finished, and bound and ready, by the weekend.

With everything completely wrapped up by Easter Sunday morning.

& I think I can do it.

As a matter of fact, I'm absolutely one hundred per cent certain that I can.

It'll be a terrific thing to leave behind.

–Ah yes! went on Wee Pat, them old falling coins of beautiful old snow. I can't tell you how much she used to love them, my own dear departed Trixie-Mae, gone now this ten years.

And then he started into telling us all about the various adventures enjoyed by himself and his wife of forty years, Trixie Mae Casey, and the good times they'd enjoyed whenever she was fit to walk the earth.

–When nothing would do the pair of us but to wander together every single winter's evening – when them sweet old flakies would be starting to show their fragile faces.

He bent his head all of a sudden and looked pained.

–Tell me, Mrs, he began, with a dry hoarseness becoming evident in his voice, where do you think she might be now? Where do you think she might have got to? For I just can't begin to tell you how I miss her. Indeed, there's never a night in our humble old cottage but I think I see her.

He faltered somewhat, gazing down at his cap.

–Well? he repeated, what would you have to say about that now, I wonder?

As he winced, ever so slightly, & my mother gently took him by the arm.

–Maybe, Wee Pat, she's up there by Our Lady's side.

–No, said Pat, I'm afraid I have to disagree – and the reason for that is that she's standing right there yonder, this very minute. With that same lovely coat with the fur trim she had on her the day we got married. Look at her there, like a sculpture carved out of snow.

Snow is various, & snow is surprising.

Snow is a ghostie-painter! I always used to think – a little light dusting and hey presto! you hear bells & you're inside a card!

Honestly, some of the things that come into your head.

Like when I'd been tossing and turning all night before finally deciding to quit all this shilly-shallying and let Mrs Beacon, once and for all, know the truth.

& with it, of course – like a lot of things, such as waiting for the dentist – it turning out to be – well, if not quite nothing – then an awful lot easier than you think.

Even though the sweat was pouring off me.

–So that's it, Mrs B, I said, I've decided once and for all it's the only way.

To get shot of old Fizzbag once and for all, I meant. Escape.

–I understand, Francie, she said – and handed me the plate.

Of scrumptious afternoon Rich Tea.

–I've always been fond of them, she said, fine tasty crunch.

As she held my hand and gave me one of her special smiles.

It was the greatest load, ever, I think, off my mind.

But then, that's always been the kind of that good old Mrs B – sort of like your mother, in that she always seems to kind of know – even before you've uttered a word.

***

Sometimes I'll just sit here chewing my pencil for hours – trying my best to capture distant days, what they felt like & that.

& not just about snow – anything at all.

This is what I came up with this morning.

'Snow Day In Annagreevy', I've called it for the moment.

```
It was coming on towards winter's end, with
not very long now to go before the arrival of
spring. As we made our way once more in the
direction of Wee Pat Casey's cottage, not far
from the glistening Annagreevy river.
    When — all of a sudden, out of nowhere —
whoosh! Why, I really could not believe my
eyes — when I beheld the most dazzling,
luxurious, swaying carpet of yellow!
```

So I had a jolly old time laying out that page – but then I decided it was time to turn in.

As I closed the computer up and made sure I had the padlock secure – because you just can't be up to what The Scuttler might do.

Although I'm well aware you can take it too far.

Sometimes I'll even get up in the night and stand at the window keeping check.

& which is stupid, yes really dumb – because all that does is wind you up into an unnecessarily vigilant state.

Just like it did this morning, round about dawn.

When I started to get nervous and say to myself: You're doing the very same thing again, fooling yourself!

& was actually on the verge of cancelling the whole thing.

The big breakout, the scarpering – however you want to describe it, I don't know.

But in the end saw sense, and managed to get back into bed for some more kip.

& then, when I got up, acting all cocky like it had never happened.

With the actual truth being that it had been a very close-run thing.

Chapter 8

The Picnic at Blackbushe

Not so very long now till the weekend – & after the holiday it will all be over.

& even though you might know that, it still doesn't prevent you from being agitated.

& which I was just now, perhaps more than ever – looking out the window to see what Ron was up to – before finally hearing the engine starting up, & the Mazda taking off down the avenue. He was telling me he was going to visit his sister in Carlow. With him no sooner having shot through the gates than I was off myself, down to the pump house to secure Madame, and have myself another good jolly practice.

Such a squeal as she made when I spun her!

As I cycled off around the back of the building, pedalling past the library and the chapel, back up by the domestic staff quarters.

I mean, honestly my friends – talk about burning rubber!

Then I went off up to see if Tom the Weaver, who I'd been meaning to consult about doing a few bits and pieces on music, had received the mag pages I sent him the other day.

I've always been very fond of The Weaver, and always will be in spite of what happened.

Because it's not his fault his brother is a bastard.

All I know is – if anyone was 'Old School', Tom the Weaver was.

With that big long greatcoat and the hair reaching down his back, that hadn't been washed in months – and you knew by looking at him that was the way he wanted it. *Who Knows Where The Time Goes?* he's always humming – the old Sandy Denny song of long ago.

You never think it can happen to you – getting old, that is.

Certainly not back in them old London days, Tom says, when he'd lived in Brixton in a squat with his 'lady', as he calls her.

He used to be Rory Gallagher's tour manager – or so he claims. 1973 was the year it all kicked off, he said.

–I guess you could say it was the very first rave in Britain, Frank. It was advertised as a Pop/Op/Costume/Fantasy-Loon/ Blowout/Drag Ball and went on the whole night – to raise funds for *The International Times*. The Softs played at it, and Pink Floyd too – there were steel bands, happenings and underground movies. It was a trip for sure, I'm telling you, when we were free as butterflies.

Whether just some of it, or any of it indeed, was true, I didn't know.

& didn't much care, to tell you the God's honest truth.

I just liked to hear him talking about it, Tommy Weaver.

I suppose because I'd always been dreaming myself of being there – in London around that time, I mean.

Instead of being doped-up here, listening to some programme about farming on the radio.

–Yeah, things were mighty cool around that time, I got to say, Frank. Did I tell you about the night I got drunk with Bobbie Dylan?

And it was while I was thinking about that that I lost control of the fucking machine, crashing the bicycle into a tree – & in the process completely buckling the whole fucking front wheel.

With the result that I had to drag it back all the way down to the pump house where I fell on top of a mountain of slack, really quite exhausted.

'London Daze' I was thinking of for Tommy's article – or 'Tommy Weaver's Musical Memories'.

If he didn't want to do it, all I had to do was tape-record it.

I mean – what a guy.

Man, could he talk.

—Let me tell you about what some folks regard as Bob the Zimmerman's greatest concert ever. It was in Blackbushe Aerodrome, Frank, a coupla hours out of London by bus. The Picnic, they called it. Graham Parker opened the show, and he played a motherfucking blistering stormer of a set. But, hardly surprisingly, all anyone wanted to hear now was Dr Bob. And when the minstrel eventually arrived on stage, I swear to God it was like he'd been beamed in specially from another world – one of no time and yet every time there ever was. So small, I'm telling you Frank, you could just about make him out and no more, got up in this top hat and preacher's frock coat. As he launches into 'Maggie's Farm' and soon everyone's going: 'Maggie! Maggie! Maggie! Out! Out! Out!' and I'm telling you, my friend, right at that moment there wasn't one present who wouldn't have taken up arms and marched directly into Downing Street. It was a sweet golden time – and we were there.

& which was something I would never be able to say – with the cold, honest truth being that around that time I had found myself confined to solitary again for punching another inmate in a fucking dispute over potatoes in the refectory.

A big long, sour drink of fucking water from Mayo – and I make no apologies, for he deserved what he got.

Especially since that was the day that they'd given me the news.

It's hard when anyone dies – but Uncle Alo, he was special.

& which was why I just sat there all day, in front of the telly – repeating his name for the benefit of no one – with everyone else out enjoying the heatwave.

& after which I'd found myself reaching the conclusion – when I'd decided that speaking to anyone was of no use any more – not now, when the uncle you loved more than anything could die in a home with no one around him.

No one to even hold his hand.

So what was the use of us loving relatives, I asked myself – or even, maybe, pretending that there was even such a thing.

Because, at the end of the day, whether you live in the same house or not, all we are in the end is only strangers.

It's funny, though, looking back – on the names that you sometimes put on things, I mean.

With Day of Uncle No-Speak being how I remember that episode now.

Having decided, quite rationally, really, as I say – that if the uncle who had meant so much to me over the course of my life could no longer speak or say anything to anyone, then neither would I.

No, neither would I.

And didn't, for a long time.

An elective mute, the doctor called it – but I don't really know, to be honest with you – more like the Gonks in your head going *mmph mmph mmph* – Gonks are named after these kind of stuffed dolls, who didn't have any bodies & were basically just heads with arms and feet. They were not very intelligent, & generally just bounced, whistled, & spoke all kinds of rubbish. They were very popular in the sixties.

Now doing their damnedest to be chatterboxes – but, with their mouths being all sewn up, not being able.

I really don't know.

I couldn't say, to be honest.

About me being an 'elective mute' and so on. But if the doctor says – then he's the boss.

Chapter 9

The Loneliness of
Emmerdale Farm

After having had a great old think about all the days I spent with Tom, I have to say that I am sorely tempted to devote an entire *Yaroo* section to him and his life and times.

& setting about dealing almost exclusively with that period, when he'd enjoyed the time of his life in the UK – as I say, when I myself was slouching around in a diazepam-induced stupor.

When Tommy the Weaver would have been the undisputed King of Brixton.

What I'd have given, just to be there.

Even for just one day, I'd told him.

–In some kind of weird way, man, you were, he'd replied. At least as far as I'm concerned, Frank.

Some of the things he used to say – they can still really somehow get to me.

–Because somewhere deep inside of them, everyone's got themselves some unique and special talent, he often said, even if they don't know what it is, or haven't found it yet. It was just a matter of keeping on searching.

–Yes, you can do it brother, he told me, nipping the tip of the Rizla as those kindly eyes squinted.

Did I mention that he had kept all his copies of the *New Musical Express*?

He had literally hundreds.

& which were just about the only things Tom the Weaver ever cared for – going literally crazy if you ever touched them without permission.

As I did that day when he caught me unawares.

–What in the name of Christ do you think you're fucking doing? Answer me, you bastard! Don't you know those magazines are exclusive and private property? How fucking well dare you, man! I mean – Jeez fucking Christ, the liberties people take!

Before stumbling off, whimpering – slamming the door of the music room behind him.

As the entire building seemed to shudder all around me.

But, as so often happened with Tom the Weaver, the following day there was nothing more about it.

I'll always remember Tom as a veritable human library of unbelievable musical facts.

Going through album after album as he described in great detail how his lady – Junie Moon, she was called – had decorated the Brixton squat in the style which reflected her taste, with big Chesterfield sofas upholstered in William Morris fabric, hand-sewn fringed covers, shawls and throws, Morris wallpaper, art nouveau posters and her collection of ceramic pots and beaded lamps.

As they sat there in a circle, slowly but beautifully dissolving, consuming yet more hashish, from the water pipe Tom had rigged up, & yet another game of stoned Scrabble was initiated.

–If only I had been there one time, I said.

If my life hadn't ended before it could properly start.

—We had always been interested in the cause of Black Power, he said, but when I met Bobby Seale I knew straight away that he was, for sure, one real special kind of soul. A beautiful black man, Frank, you know? I really dug what he had to say. We stayed for a week in his pad in Hamburg but then he went back to LA for a rally. So me and Junie, we just hung out. We'd had a bust up, you see, with this dude Wolfgang that we'd met. A kind of bad spirit, you know what I'm trying to say? It really got on my nerves eventually. So we didn't have no choice but to part company. I couldn't stand the sight of him, actually, in the end. So what if I hit him? He was trying to rip us off.

It was at times like that that you wouldn't really know what to think – with Tom suddenly getting up and starting to walk around, opening and closing his fists as he muttered away to himself.

—I don't know if you ever actually heard of Sandy Denny, did you Frank? There's a photo of her here on the front of the *NME* – she used to play with the band Fairport Convention.

& it's hard not to think of Sandy dropping by their Brixton squat, unannounced – kneeling on the carpet & rolling a number – with herself & Junie in their velvet Elizabethan-style floor-length gowns, going through the Tarot or sewing patterned cushions.

With this plump Tabby sitting there looking across at them.

—*Who knows where the time goes?*

That was probably his masterpiece, Tom the Weaver.

Because he was a really great guitarist as well.

& I sometimes think I can still hear him play.

Memories like that – when they hit, they can come close to breaking you.

Especially when they arrive completely out of nowhere.

I don't know why it ought to have made me think about Ma
— remembering Tom when he played that tune.

But it did.

With her turning the corner, as large as life, strolling along in
her frock coat behind the pram.

—Oh that Bunny Cuddles! How is he doing, my prince,
down there? she says.

Bending down to give me a taste of strawberry jam on a spoon.

—Just an ickle spoonful.

I could taste it so vividly that it might not have been a memory at all.

Although it was late, there were still pockets of children
playing — pinging pebbles against the marble bowl of the
Victorian fountain.

Covering their ears & scrunching up their eyes — waiting for
the inevitable ricochet.

—Yip yip yip! they'd squeal, in a circle.

It was great.

But that, unfortunately, was when the scene began to
change — and I found myself, suddenly, back in the house where
I'd been born.

Where it was deadly quiet.

&, like I mean — real fucking quiet.

As though someone were on the point of dying.

Someone you knew.

Already the neighbours had begun to arrive — shaking their
umbrellas, mute as they assembled in the hall, doffing hats &
removing greatcoats.

Music was playing on the old valve radio.

—*Silver bells, silver bells, it's Christmastime in the city*, Bing
Crosby crooned softly.

As, gradually, they entered the kitchen – hesitantly, in single file, much more subdued than ever I remembered.

They were all the people from my home town – almost everyone I'd ever known, in fact – with their faces shockingly lucid in the moonlight.

Then the parlour door opened – & there, standing over by the polished mahogany cabinet, were my father and mother.

& alongside them, my uncle who was dead.

& who looked like a corpse, but in every other way the exact same as when he'd been alive – in a suit of herringbone tweed, with his trademark little triangle of red hankie in the breast pocket.

–This is dreadful news, someone said, the worst ever.

–This house is haunted – everyone here knows that, someone else, quite dispassionately, observed.

–But then, how could we, honestly, expect it to be otherwise? said someone else.

After that, no one else said anything and they all just stood there – listening to the strains of *Friday Night Is Music Night* ebbing and swelling through the chevron of the radio's fretted baize.

Until, suddenly, & really quite alarmingly, the back door slammed and the parish priest fell in, his shoulders covered in a light cape of snow.

He was close to weeping as he wrung his hands.

–There's no justice, said one of the neighbours.

–It's not for us to understand, said someone else.

As the muffled sound of fluttering temporarily disturbed the air – and they looked up to see a robin at the window.

–I've come to deliver a message, it chirped.

& one of the ladies burst out crying.

Then the robin flapped noiselessly onto the top of the piano – before releasing a piercing, agonised squeal – and they gazed in dazed dread as a bead-sized spot of blood hung suspended from the underside of its beak.

After which, its trill proved quite unbearable.

—A white blinding light known only in dreams heretofore will soon annihilate everything in its path. And the reason for that is the presence of a murderer – because of what he has done. The one of whom I speak is known to you all – and his iniquities have separated him from his creator. Yes, from whom God has forever turned His face. Goodnight to you all.

The kitchen was empty.

As I found myself shooting forward in the chair, realising where I was, and where it was I'd been all along – in the recreation room, watching *Emmerdale* on the TV.

& whose music now sounded like the loneliest theme on earth.

Making me think of the house disappearing, with the walls and all falling down without a sound, and everyone in it vanished forever.

As I stood there alone, on some kind of moor – an ageless landscape of leafless trees, with not a single habitation in sight.

I've never heard anything like that surging theme tune – even yet, it can make me shiver.

Because what it is is the sound of that stretching moorland, the very essence of that place – sootish, carbonated.

With that pale, familiar, unbroken prospect and a slot of white where the only thing audible in the world is the wind.

That sees you, once again, placing one foot in front of the other.

Knowing in your heart that what you're doing is fruitless.

Because wherever it is you're going – or wherever it is you might think you're headed – you're never going to get here.

—I fucking loves this, bro'! I heard Ricky Shabs calling from across the room, swinging his legs on the arm of the settee as he finished off what was left of his chips.

As, just like at the opening of the programme, the grey Land Cruiser went on ploughing determinedly through the countryside, restlessly churning the rough mud of Emmerdale Farm.

& what I would have given just not to be there any more – to cease without ceremony, right there on the spot – for my heart, ever so quietly, to simply neglect performing its appointed function.

Chapter 10

Niki Lauda

Dear Readers

I hope you enjoy this latest instalment of what has proved to be one of our most popular features: 'What Would You Do?'

Well, I'm sure as we all know, the answer differs from individual to individual. But, make no mistake, for each and every one of us, the decision depends on split-second timing.

How, for instance, would you react if you happened to be a rally driver forced off a road into a river, with there being no chance to jump out of the car before it plunges into deep waters, where the pressure of water will be too strong for the driver or his passenger to force open the doors?

Or, perhaps, if you were a lumberjack trapped in a raging forest fire, with the roaring flames cutting you off from safety?

Or maybe you have escaped from a blazing plane only to find you have crash-landed in a swamp, which is slowly sucking you down deeper and deeper …

I was in the middle of putting the finishing touches to that article and trying to find some suitable action-packed illustrations on the web to accompany it, when I hear a light knock and look up to see Cecil, standing there yoo-hoo and all the rest.

—Ah there you are, Francis, he says with a smile, hard at it as usual. And do you know what I'm going to tell you, my old friend? I don't think I've ever seen you look so happy!

But I knew he was only saying that as a means of lifting my spirits – seeing as he'd arrived with the details about the funeral.

I didn't want to say it – but Tom the Weaver, he died you see. & it was me who found him.

& which shows you – it's all very well saying what you'd do, whether it's with a crocodile in your canoe or the failure of the atomic motors in your spaceship – but till it actually happens, you just don't know.

As the two of us just sat there, staring out the window of my little garden hut, and knowing that we both were thinking the very same things – about Tom & his antics, that we'd never see again.

It was like he'd arrived, for a moment, and sat between us – staring from in behind that long lank curtain of hair, with the roll-up pinched between two trembling fingers.

—I'll be seeing her soon, Junie Moon, I heard him say, did I ever tell you about her career as an artist? Oh my Junie, what a wonder.

—She'd been working on a book of children's illustrations, he went on, based on Patricia Lynch's *The Turf Cutter's Donkey*.

—I just can't wait to talk to her about it, he said, because that was her dream, before we broke up. To be a famous children's author, you know?

Then he stared down at the floor.

—Maybe there won't be any smack in heaven, he said, because that's what ruined it between us in the end. It wasn't me and her. I swear to you, Frank. Fuck that skag, and everything that it did.

They had always wanted to open a restaurant – a wholefood place.

–The Golden Dawn, we were going to call it.

& which was exactly what I had been thinking, that day when I found him down at the pump house. Maybe some day we would all enter upon some blissful golden …

–Tommy? I remember calling – I'd seen him going in there – as I pushed the door open.

& then closed it gently behind me again as I did my best to pick my way through all the debris that was lying around in there, tripping over an old broken pram.

Then I heard the groaning in the dark.

–I'm going to die, said Tom the Weaver. Frank is that you? I'm sorry, man. I really & truly am. Without Junie I'm nothing.

It was one of those industrial-style plastic bottles, kind of like Domestos – but when I lifted it, I saw that it was empty. I could just about make out the label in the gloom:

Gramoxone SL 2.0 cdms, net
Restricted use

Me & Big Brains were the only ones let out to attend the funeral – thanks, of course, to the committed & persistent interventions of Dr Cecil.

& even that wasn't easy – but he'd be too decent to ever tell you that.

All I can say is that I apologise for any embarrassment caused – because it wasn't meant to happen.

The trouble between Tommy's brother and me.

Not when he was related to a very close friend and old buddy of mine – and definitely, most definitely, not at a funeral.

But you can blame that fucker Denny for that – spoiling for a scrap from the start so he was, right from that very first second when I spotted him staring over, after he'd seen me in the yard of the church.

Ah fuck him – because he isn't worth it.

Although I'd like to know what he'd have to say if you came up behind him and shouted out:

–Hey Denny! What would you do if you fell in a vat of warm bubbling jam?

& then, just when he's turning round to see who's asking such a stupid dumb question, go:

SPLAT!

With a great big fistful of good warm mush right there in that great big fat old Denny kisser!

Oh, man, what a laugh.

It amused me so much that I carried on writing my column – all about what would you do, only this time all mixed up with facts concerning jam.

& which I happen to know quite a lot about, if you please.

Mainly thanks to my adventures long ago in a certain principality named Town of Strawberry.

I'll never forget it as long as I live. Especially when you decide to set off on your humble little bockety conveyance, namely a busted old ladies' bike, as you make your way far away from your old home town, optimistically travelling to the reaches of a neighbouring county – piloting your trusty ship-of-the-road in the direction of Newtownbutley – much-fabled in my mind as ye olde celebrated Village of Jam, where the principal manufacturing plant of New Carn Preserves was proudly located.

Although much was also made of its reputation for raising chickens.

With much burble-burbling continuing as I approached, perhaps as many as four or five great rocket-shaped silos rose up out of the mist – for all the world like our own little humble Cuba.

'Welcome to Newtown' read the neatly painted sign as I made my approach on my humble little bicycle.

This was twenty or thirty or forty years ago, maybe more.

I was glad to be visiting – for, so far as I could see, in many respects it was a fine old district, every inch the equal of my own well-regarded birthplace.

& to which I had made my way for the purpose of collecting fruit for payment – yes, gathering all the raspberries you could get your hands on and dropping them into the bottom of a specially provided wicker basket.

Or punnet, as it was called.

& for which you were to be paid a tanner, amounting to six old pennies, for every pound of fruit that you picked – by no means a bad transaction in those times.

So off I went to the jam fields, armed with my punnet.

This is a grand old place, this Newtown, I reflected.

Or at least it was on that very first day – subsequent to which, I am sorry to have to report, things took a decided turn for the worse.

When some hoodlums, their actions directed principally by an individual named Skin 'Store-Calf' McElligott – elected to take exception to my presence.

Not that this, in any respect, proved difficult – because all that was necessary in those days to attract unwelcome attention was, quite simply, to be a native of some town or parish, which wasn't Newtown.

This would be more than sufficient for considerable violence to be visited upon your person.

& which didn't take long, as I was soon to discover – in the aftermath of a dispute, finding myself suspended by the heels, upside down in a copper vat of steaming blackberry jam pulp.

As a charge sheet containing a list of purported offences was laboriously & flamboyantly read out by Store-Calf, most notable among them the act of spying on the nips of Henry Mulligan's sister. Henry was among his dear & closest friends, he asserted. & all this in spite of the fact that, at such a tender age – I had barely turned ten – I scarcely knew what nips were, or were for.

Although it must be admitted that I had, & for some considerable period of time, enjoyed the view of which he spoke – & which had been unexpectedly presented to me through a fortuitous parting in the high hedge adjoining mine.

As Store-Calf's sister – whose name, as I recall, was Puddeners, released intermittent falsetto peals of ever-increasing passion.

–Oh Christ! I heard her moan, oh man, dear God, that's great, do it again Shamey!

As I abandoned my little wicker basket and, filled with the prospect of further entanglements, sank to one knee and gave my complete attention to that region of her anatomy – which in themselves, it occurred to me, resembled nothing so much as a brace of bruised, distended raspberries.

–Oh Shamey how I love you! Puddeners McElligott squealed as she gripped the bushes, oh that is so fucking powerful I can't tell you!

And, after that:

–Oh Shamey, my love – do you really mean it?

Before, to my dismay, I looked up to find myself surrounded.

–Ho, boys! We have him now! bawled Store-Calf, rushing forward – as I found myself hauled through a jungle of ragwort, thistles & briars.

–This is the end for you! he kept saying, there's no doubt about it – you've been caught red-handed now, you dirty skitter – spying on women, you ought to be ashamed!

–Especially when it's my sister! shouted up Henry Mulligan.

–That's right! agreed Store-Calf, for a fellow to do the like of that! There is only one punishment for him, I'm sorry to say.

I've had it now, I remember thinking and, sure enough, I was right – I had.

With the reading of the charge sheet being the last thing I remember as I dangled there, hopelessly, face down in what was effectively a giant ocean of jam.

A veritable Loch Ness of mashed-up fruit.

As, far away, my assailants laughed their heads off – cautioning me that if I ever so much as dared, in their lifetime, to ever even think about approaching the 'sweet wee town of Newtownbutley' again – much less spy on people's private and personal nipples in through bushes – what I found myself experiencing at this moment would be as nothing compared with what was in store.

As off they went, grunting, and climbing robustly on one another's backs.

***

So those were my adventures in what came to be known as the Town of Strawberry.

& all I can say is – what my poor mother must have thought whenever she looked up and saw me arriving at the back door in such a wretched, woebegone state – having literally sloshed like a monster up the lane and into our yard. White as a ghost, she was, and I wouldn't blame her.

& which I only bother mentioning, at this point at all, as a result of it being just about the only thing I remember from the day of Tom the Weaver's funeral. Which had been so awful in almost every respect that that little daydream, or reverie, or whatever you want to call it – the briefest of reminiscences, I suppose – was the only worthwhile memory that I have of a truly fucking rotten occasion.

& if that's why they thought I was smiling – not taking it seriously, like Denny Weaver said – then so be it.

I mean what the fuck does Denny Weaver know?

Because everyone's entitled to their own private thoughts.

But not me, apparently.

Because of what I've done in the past.

Yes, look at him over there: Frank fucking you-know-who.

& we all know what he did, don't we, ladies & gentlemen.

Oh yes.

What are they letting him come in here for?

The likes of him doesn't belong in a church.

Oh is that a fact, Denny Weaver?

Is that an absolute fact, do you tell me?

Mr Denny fuckface Weaver.

Who, quite coincidentally, had actually been the very first person I'd encountered in the churchyard – &, straight away, I could feel his eyes all over me.

Eyes that said:

–We know all there is to know about you – so don't go thinking we don't. Yes, just be careful & mind your manners. You got that, Frank? You got that, Mr So-Called-Friend-of-My-Brother's?

As if he's gonna pal around with the likes of you. Because my brother had class.

So that was a nice thing to hear on the morning of a funeral, wasn't it?

However, so be it, I said, kneeling down.

I know what you're thinking – that I might just as well have imagined those 'eyes' – because people generally don't behave like that. Not on solemn occasions, at least rarely. And, I know – you'd like to think so.

But I know what I saw.

& which was why I tried to distract myself – by remembering stories such as the one about the nips and the jam.

Sad to say, it didn't work, however.

Because, at least three times, he elbowed his friend and they both turned around.

Then he leaned across and whispered:

–Frank.

It was years since I'd heard it murmured in that way.

& it made me sick.

Because I thought I'd left it all – all of that behind.

Seemingly not, I'm sorry to have to say.

& that was, more or less, the lead-up to what happened that day – the accident, or whatever you want to call it.

Even just thinking about the two of them makes me nauseous & want to heave – but Denny himself, more than his friend.

Because the way I saw it – who was he to stand in judgement over me?

Especially considering his past & background, which, 'class' or not, Tommy himself had told me all about.

The poor man's an alcoholic, he'd said, no matter how he tries he just can't seem to kick the juice.

No, I thought as I fiddled with a prayer book, far too busy turning around to look at other people who are no fucking business of his and saying things about them.

Such as they murder and give people cheek.

–He likes to make a laugh of things. Tell you things, stories maybe about jam. But you and me know only too well what he's capable of. Don't we?

–Oh yes, nodded the friend, we do indeed, Denny. We know that for sure.

So there you have it – that was more or less the lead up.

And, to tell you the truth, looking back on it now, I really wish it had never happened.

Not out of any sympathy I might have for Denny Weaver – but, in spite of myself, it somehow tainted not only the day of the funeral itself but the special memory that I had of Tom.

As I kept on wondering – would he forgive me?

Or, worse – even understand?

& I still don't know.

That is – I can't be sure.

As well as that, there was the effect it had on The Professor.

Whatever he was on, I think they had to double the dosage after.

But, without trying to get myself off the hook, I really have to say that it hadn't helped me – with him sniffling all the way through the service.

& squeezing my arm real hard – I mean you should have seen the bruises! – as he kept on pushing the hankie into his face & repeating he's gone, he's gone, poor old Thomas yes he's gone!

Forever now, Frank.

Frank now, forever.

& I think it was then that Denny had turned around – curling his lip in that appalling, accusing way.

As if to say: I wouldn't be surprised if it was you who killed him.

I'd been able to laugh it off at first.

&, indeed, the second time – by wandering off and thinking about the Store-Calf, Henry Mulligan and his sister.

But the third time – no.

When he curled the lip:

–You don't think we don't know?

Then when you'd look again, he'd be gone – leafing through the pages of his missal, with the woman in black to his side holding his arm.

It was all very clever.

Because who could ever confront him directly.

& all I can say is, it made me sad.

With it all having taken place in a church, as much as anything.

In search of comfort, I leaned back against the green mottled pillar situated directly behind me.

It was pleasantly cool to the touch and had the effect of calming me down considerably, I'm happy to be able to say.

& it's a pity it was then that I heard it again – clear as a bell, & after that there was no going back.

In spite of him making a great show of cupping his hand as he whispered it to his friend, regrettably just as soon as he opened his mouth, I knew that already it was all over.

–How come he was first on the scene? That sounds pretty suspicious to me.

–I'm sorry that it had to be your brother, agreed the friend, but knowing what we're dealing with, it doesn't come as any surprise.

No, no surprise at all, I repeated.

& wanted to vomit.

So, faced with that – ask yourself the question:

What would you do?

***

Looking back now, of course, Denny Weaver is extremely lucky he wasn't killed.

Because as soon as the cable of the Citroën snapped, he had completely & utterly lost control of the vehicle.

With all I can remember after that being knots of mourners dressed in white & black coming running across the churchyard, with the hats of the women blowing off in the wind.

They were in a right old state.

As they forced the door open and managed to get him out in one piece – leading him into the chapel like a cripple.

Although, in fact, he hadn't been seriously physically hurt.

It was a good old plan, though.

Even if I do say so myself.

You see the minder looking after me, half the time he wasn't there at all, and whenever I motioned towards the sign GENTLEMEN, I don't even think he noticed me doing it at all.

So in I went, and was out through the skylight in a second – and back in my seat alongside him before he knew it.

But I think, more than anything about that master plan, what gave me the greatest sense of satisfaction was the fact that I'd used Tommy's weapon to do it – the Swiss Army knife I'd unexpectedly found in his pocket that terrible day in the pump house.

I suppose I just wanted something to remember him by.

And now, here it was – being put to good use already.

So – snip! it went, neatly – Denny Weaver's famous Citroën brake cable.

& there I am, being interviewed by police.

Although, honest to God, detectives these days – are they worth a damn?

It was all a long way from Edgar Wallace, I kept thinking, & my old favourite: *The Clue of the Twisted Candle.*

–He was the closest and most wonderful friend that I've ever known, Tommy the Weaver, I told them.

And which isn't, & wasn't – and never will be – a lie.

But they kept on looking at me.

Then who do we meet in the corridor after the interrogation.

–Ah good man, Denny! I declared, shoving out the paw the minute I seen him.

With the next thing you know, before you can say aye or boo, the whispering fucker he's away off round the corner.

–Come back here, Denny! I shouts out and start laughing.

As one of the trusty 'tecs gives me a dig.

The Scuttler, of course, wasn't long hearing about the shenanigans.

–I know why poor auld Woolly Creegan lost his job, he growled – meaning my minder – and him with a wife and three small childer to support.

–Yes, I know. It's a sad old state of affairs, there's no mistake!

–The leopard never changes his spots! I heard him calling back as he went off, trundling his barrow, that's one sure thing you can be certain of in this world – but we're onto you, Brady, and we'll watch you like a hawk. You just make sure and be assured about that.

–Ah go on to hell, you long-nosed effing auld drink of water! I shouted after him.

Although, in retrospect, I really don't know what all the fuss and commotion was about – I mean, it wasn't like it was a case for The Sweeney.

I mean, Denny Weaver was shaken, yes, but not disfigured or even badly hurt – and certainly not killed.

Although it did make me laugh whenever he came back to the hospital for Tommy's things and I called out 'Niki Lauda!' whenever I seen him coming.

& then away off down the corridor, white as a ghost, dropping books and socks and whatnot.

Only for Cecil, I was looking at two years' solitary at least.

Because he didn't think I did it – even if I did.

So there you are – what is anyone to think of that?

Yes, just what would we do without the likes of Dr Cecil, Fizzbag's most famous clinical director ever?

& who, right from the very first day he came strolling in through the gates, has always been 120 per cent on my side – unlike certain people who prefer to spread rumours – and if that's not bad enough, doing so by leaning over and whispering to friends when they're in a church.

May he lie in peace, my old friend Tommy Weaver.

God rest his precious, much-missed soul.

Chapter 11

The Russians, the Russians, the Russians Aren't Coming

Donald Trump is everywhere these days – with the big talk recently being whether or not him and Putin were involved in a conspiracy.

& which may or may not be true, but so far as I'm concerned they can do what they fucking like, for I've just about had it up to here with Russians – from Cuba right up to the present day, which I'll tell you about later on.

But I will say this – if it does turn out that poor old Trump is involved, I hope for his sake he knows what he's doing.

With the main reason for that being that Vladimir used to work for the KGB – and if you're taking on them, just make sure you stay away from poisoned umbrellas, not to mention nerve agents being discovered in your food.

Did you know that he sometimes wrestles bears?

A right old fruit & nutcase, if you ask me.

Which is exactly what they used to say, in the old days, about Nikita Khrushchev – with all his warheads trained on New York City.

–Well that's it then! We've been given our last orders, & there's nothing for it now but to put our faith in the man above, they'd tell you.

Before heading off up to the church to fling themselves down in front of the altar with the sweat rolling off them and their lips flittering away as if their very lives depended on it – which, when you think about it, they probably did.

At least where Hughie 'Kerensky' Mackleson of The Terrace was concerned.

& who, if he happened to be alive today, most likely would be employed by NASA.

Coming puffing along in his painter's overalls, figuring out puzzles and equations and formulae with a pencil – until, just as soon as he seen you, hauling you into a shop doorway, pressing an index finger to his lips & looking suspiciously all around him.

Before proceeding on to inform you that there wasn't any need to be worried about what was 'coming'.

Because he had been extremely busy over the past few weeks, he went on, and had everything looked after for 'the time', as he described it.

Meaning, of course, the nuclear holocaust, which was imminent – now only a matter of days.

& then letting you in on a 'very special secret' – that he had just completed the construction of his own personal fallout shelter – located underneath his shed at the back of The Terrace.

And explaining, furthermore, that on account of you being a mannerly and admirably upstanding 'young cub', the least he could do was treat you to a private and 'top secret' personal tour of his impregnable concrete fortress – just this week completed.

& which had turned out, as it happened, to be a most impressive physical structure – took my breath away, indeed.

He had followed the instruction manual to the letter, he told me, and managed to finish 'the whole fucking shebang' in a matter of weeks.

–Because time is of the essence, he said, shaking his head, after all did the man himself, the president of the USA, John F. Kennedy – did he not speak of a pressing need that is 'new to our shores'?

–Did he not say that? he said, as he looked straight at me.

I said I didn't know.

–It's a matter of emergency preparedness now, said Kerensky, and if you're left without a bunker, then don't say you weren't warned. And don't let them tell you that they're just not fit to afford it – because, what with this being the modern era, there are all kinds of pay and purchase plans available to everyone – with shelters and bunkers to suit every pocket. And I'm telling you now that no family can afford to be without one – seeing as its definite that, any day now, the Cold War is destined to turn hot. And very hot indeed, might I add.

Look at this, he said, it's a fold-up bed.

As a divan suddenly appeared, swinging away out from the wall – and back in again, just as quick.

–Do you see this wooden support up here, young Frank? Just let Comrade Khrushchev come over here and try tossing that. And these walls over yonder, do you remark them? Six inches of pure cement – yes, solid massed concrete is what you're dealing with here, my lad. So come on ahead then, Nikita – let's be having you, you traitorous, no-good Russki. Come on right over and try to blow up the town. Let's be having all the rockets you can fire. But would you like to know something? OK then, Nikita – listen to me and listen very carefully. Because what you are doing is wasting your precious time, you baldy old bastard. You see, over here, I have enough tinned food stockpiled to last me and herself and the kiddies for, at the very least, eighteen months. You weren't expecting that, I'm sure! However, hold up there for a bit – for now it's time for us to perform our drill.

As he clicked his heels and gave the salute.

–The radioactive dust, he started up again, this fatal cloud – it can threaten us citizens in three different ways – we must try to avoid each of these dangers, he explained.

Before suddenly releasing an unmerciful roar:

–STAYING INDOORS IS THE ONLY ANSWER!

He also said it was important that I inform my parents – and to keep the radio on all night, ensuring it was tuned to the national station, Radio Éireann.

–Have you got that? he said, in an English sergeant-major accent.

I nodded and said I had.

–When you hear the FINAL WARNING, you will know that all-out war has started and that the town, as we know it, is now more or less fucked. If you have fires in grates or boilers, extinguish them. Turn off your water supply at the stopcock and any gas or electric water heaters in use. Yellow flags along roads will indicate FINAL WARNING to motorists and other road users.

He snapped the book closed and tucked it smartly beneath his arm.

–Well? he enquired. Any questions, soldier?

–No Sir, I replied, no Sir, major.

–Very good, Frank Brady. Stand down, if you please.

And, as we stood there admiring his creation in every aspect, there could clearly be no argument that whenever it came to not only the construction of uniquely impregnable fallout shelters, Hughie 'Kerensky' Mackleson was triumphantly out on his own.

Not that it made a great deal of difference in the end.

For what did baldy old Khrushchev do?

Only went and fucked off, forgetting all about Cuba and everywhere else.

–Like every politician down the ages, as The Professor says, for all we are is pawns in their game.

Before then, as usual, going and forgetting all about it, delivering a commentary on the football match of his dreams – when he and his missus went off to see Kerry playing Cavan in New York, in the All-Ireland Final of 1947.

A cloud of midges hovered above his head – as he struck them a blow and tried intercepting an imaginary ball coming sailing down out of the air.

–Here in New York we're now halfway through the second half – and into the square comes a high-dropping ball.

Then, all of a sudden, he completely loses interest & sits back down with his head in his hands.

–Who am I? he asks me then.

–Sometimes I wish I could just die right here and now. Because all that seems to remain of me is some badly acted version of myself that I don't recognise. Who is he? And what is he doing, playing out these versions of me – maybe trying to help me to find my way back to who I was when I was young, before it happened.

Then what happens, he starts chuckling again & talking about Donald Trump & counting out various trouble spots on his fingers.

–Egypt, Aleppo, the Congo – and today Mexico. He's separating children from their parents now. Even Hitler wasn't as bad as that. Come on Cavan – you can do it. Send those Kerrymen back to the hills!

–I have to go now, Professor, I said.

As off I went, doing my best not to think about Russians.

& not of the Kerensky variety, either, I'm sorry to have to say.

Because it was them – believe it or not, as Jack Palance would say! – who were responsible for the abject failure of my first big breakout from Fizzbag all those many long years ago.

On the night of the collapse of the Twin Towers in NY – I mean, I ask you!

What a time to pick, I swear, to stage an escape.

But that's what happened.

Although I have to say that it's funny now when you think about it.

Especially when they weren't Russians at all.

The Russians, the Russians, the Russians – aren't coming!

It's hard to believe that it's all of seventeen years.

But, like Joe Friday used to say: those are the facts.

Just the facts, ma'am!

–Once upon a time, a certain long-stay inmate by the name of Frank from Fizzbag made a hopeless attempt to escape from confinement and wound up getting battered for his pains! By a bunch of no-good criminals who turned out not to be Russians!

Yes, sad to say, the fuckers who ended up being responsible for my recapture, they turned out not to be from anywhere near Russia or the fucking Ukraine, like I'd thought.

But I'll tell you all about that later.

Just make sure you know this – it isn't going to happen like that this time.

Nope, no Sir.

Because this escape is planned right down to the very letter.

With nothing – but nothing! – being left to chance.

Because I've learned my lesson – so roll on Easter!

Read all about it in *The Big Yaroo*. Francie Brady busts out at last!

The only one I'll really miss, to be honest, is Mary – because she really is the loveliest woman, Mrs Beacon.

Let's face it – it's not every day you're diagnosed with cancer – and she was there to hold my hand.

It's surprising, all the same, how quickly you can get used to it.

& of course, she's been through it herself, Mrs B.

With her little cat Toddy – who's, apparently, been very poorly.

–Hopefully, this time your tests will come out clear, she'd said, driving me out to Blanch in her car.

Sad to report, however, they weren't.

–I'll storm heaven, she says.

& I liked that a lot –my mother used to say it.

Storm heaven.

I used to like repeating it to myself.

I don't know what I'd have done without her.

Because, in fact, she reminds me of the way that things used to be.

Before everything went so horribly wrong and my Ma had drowned herself in the lake along with the rats.

That time when unhappiness came to reside inside my heart like it owned it – along with vengeance and bitterness, and one or two other kinds of feelings I can't name.

Because I don't know how, and which sometimes make me want to cry:

–Yaroo! Yaroo-oo-oo-oo fucking-oo!

Except that I can't seem to manage to do that, either.

Because it just goes and dies there, deep in the pit of your stomach, long before it gets anywhere near your throat.

I wonder how Mrs Beacon's cat is now.

Ray is his favourite kind of fish of them all, she says.

–My own wee Toddy Ray, she'll say, and you'd nearly think she was talking about her husband.

Chapter 12

Teatime with Tommy

In terms of knowledge and sheer all-round intelligence, there is no one – at least not in my experience – who has ever passed through the gates of Fizzbag who could compare with The Professor.

At least, that is, whenever he isn't 'doting'.

Which is what they used to always call his problem whenever I was young.

It's like being outside of a lighted window looking in, watching your whole life being played out by someone else, he says.

–With all the amazing facts you know, you're better than any computer, I told him.

And do you know what he said?

–The Australian Scientific and Industrial Research Department says that if we don't do something soon hundreds of acres of what should have been golden wheat fields in Queensland will very shortly turn into desert.

–Thanks, I told him, I'll remember that.

Folding his arms as he leaned across and picked a leaf off a branch of the linden.

There really doesn't seem to be anything he doesn't know about.

& I told him that.

But he just shook his head and sighed.

–Maybe I do but it's all mixed up. What happens is I'm going to say something – and then, without warning, I find that I take a sharp left on the landing and the next thing you know I'm in the lighted room.

–I see, I said.

–And that's when I see them – almost anyone I've ever known throughout the course of my life. Except I don't know them – or who it is they're supposed to be!

He patted the thin listless strands on his head.

& then started to put on a kind of play – he does that a lot.

This one concerned his father – or a version of him.

–What a wonderful man, he moaned, and I almost wept.

Because, you see, it reminded me of my own.

It was like the two of us had been travelling back in time.

–I want you to write an article for me, for the magazine. About history.

He didn't know the first thing about technology, he said, or for that matter publishing – but would, nonetheless, be honoured to accept the commission.

– 'A Professor Remembers', I suggested as a possible title.

–Very good, he replied, a very good choice. Why, I really cannot wait to get started.

As off he went, wiggling his fingers behind his back, rapt in thought.

So you can imagine my excitement two or three days later – I was going over some editorial items with Fr Ron on the computer – when the knock came to the door and we looked around to see a small white square of paper being slid underneath, followed by the sound of hastily retreating footsteps.

With the very first thing that I seen at the top being Muggsy's name. And, directly underneath:

A Professor Remembers:

As I felt my stomach churn with the most delicious of excitements – simply because I knew how good it was likely to be.

Before I saw, scrawled, in heavy red biro ink:

A Professor Remembers: prostitutes, I wonder would you **please** go off about your business and ply your trade somewhere else. **Thank you.**

I really didn't know what to say – and neither did the clergyman.

So I just quietly folded the little white square and left it down by the side of the computer.

As the padre tugged his cuff and swallowed hard.

–I rather fancy a cup of tea, he suggested.

And we never did refer to 'the note' again.

Come to that, neither did The Professor.

As we carried on with our usual conversations – about this and that, football and drama, and the hopes that I had for my 'periodical' as he called it.

–Ah yes! The Professor chortled, Michael Collins always said that my father, God rest him, was as keen a shot as any Boer sniper – and that the Tommies, for sure, had sure met their match in him.

Then I looked up to see The Scuttler – standing with his barrow, staring right over directly at me.

–What are they giving you a computer for, he said, you that can neither read nor write?

I lifted a rock that was lying underneath the bench and sent it skimming right past his ear.

–Jesus! he bawled.

But he needn't have worried – for I'd have hit him if I wanted.

Then he took off, falling halfway across the barrow, before stopping by the sundial to shout back:

—You big useless tub of lard. I have the goods on you, and I'll blow! You just see if I don't, you fat fuck!

Then when I looked again he was gone, with a turnip rolling after him down along the grassy slope.

—Then there's the other thing, I heard The Professor say.

—What's that, I said, Prof?

And then he just looks at me, as if though I'd never been born or existed, which is the way I often feel, sometimes, myself.

—Good evening, he says, you're all very welcome to *Teatime with Tommy*.

Which is a programme that used to be on years ago, with Tommy the host tinkling away on the keyboard before turning as he smiled at the camera and read out another musical request.

Although I've only actually seen it once or twice myself.

& which is so long ago that I sometimes think I might even have made it up – so good was the day, or should I say, the evening, that I spent in its glow with probably the best people in the town, if not even the world, that I grew up in.

& where you wouldn't have expected me to be, at least most people wouldn't.

Because that was the way things were in those days.

Back in 'them times', as Wee Pat used to say.

—Long before auld breakouts or bucking magazines were ever thought of! you can almost hear him add, as he sits there on his gate – with some old sheep or cow looking over his shoulder, angling to get maybe a handful of nuts, or sugar or something.

Anyway, what happened this day was that the teacher in the school had said to us boys, what I want is for you to write me a composition – and what it's to be called is 'My Most Unforgettable Day'.

And, after that, said it was to be like 'My Most Unforgettable Character', which I knew you could find in the *Reader's Digest*, seeing as my father always used to get it.

But the teacher went ahead and read it to us anyway, & saying all the time that it was just to give us an idea.

Yes, around every month or so, a copy used to come for my father in the post – but he wasn't the only one in the town who read it.

Oh, most certainly not – for I knew there were twelve or perhaps even thirteen or fourteen of them, all lined up in a row on Mr Nugent's bookcase in his sitting room – with the light shining on their green and pale-blue spines. So he must have belonged to the same club as my father.

Well, you should have seen the face of the teacher when I handed in my essay.

–I'm afraid I don't know what's going on in your head, Brady! he said.

As all the others looked around as if to say: very well then, what's your explanation?

But I said nothing – just sat down.

& that was the end of it – for them, at least.

&, I suppose, the teacher.

Not that he was mad or anything.

Far from it.

Because I think he was even glad that I did anything!

Anyway, I was happy – because what happened then was that my two best friends in the world, Joe & Philip – they had actually shared the prize.

For the 'Big Essay Comp of the Year 1960', as it was called.

I think the award was two-and-six.

Or half a dollar, as they used to call it then.

With which they purchased a bagful of Cough-No-Mores.

They gave me three.

So was it any wonder it'd be your most unforgettable day?

Especially since it had really only started.

With, as I say, the popular programme *Teatime with Tommy*
only just beginning on the television in the warm and cosy Nugent
family living room — with the small screen in the corner shedding
its smoky white glow just as we came wandering in.

To be met by the sound of Philip's mother rattling crockery
out in the kitchen.

&, believe it or not — she was singing.

Yes, lilting away to herself inside — don't ask me what, for I
didn't happen to know the tune.

But I will tell you this — I know it was happy.

—This is the very first time I've been in here, I said to Philip.

—Yes, I know, he said, as he flicked back his tie and knelt
down on the carpet.

Philip and that old stripy tie — how good he looked, I remembered thinking, him and his school cap and socks — and, of course,
that lovely special crested blazer.

This is the happiest day of my life, I kept on thinking — but
making sure not to say it too loudly or enthusiastically — in case
by doing that, you'd make it disappear.

As Joe came over and said:

—Here's the Snakes & Ladders.

He often played them now with Philip — I know because he
told me.

& glory be, here I was — kneeling right in between the two
of them.

How did this happen?

Amazing.

That was all you could say about it.

With ring boards here and boxes of Ludo there — not to mention blow-football and Scalextric.

It was difficult not to choke seeing as you found yourself so happy.

Then what happens – the front door doesn't it open, and who comes in in his topcoat, only Mr Nugent carrying something.

Which, in fact, turned out to be a great big brown-wrapped box. A present!

Philip was beside himself tearing off the wrapping.

He was like a man gone mad, ripping the papers off in flitters, which wasn't something you expected him to do.

With none of us being able to open our mouths to try and so much as utter a word – just as soon as we saw what was inside the box.

As Philip Nugent's father came over to help him with its arms.

The arms, that is, of Captain Troy Tempest – supreme submarine commander of Marineville.

–Stand by for action! Anything can happen in the next half hour! I heard Joe Purcell call out in ecstasy.

Because that was what you heard at the beginning of the *Stingray* programme.

Before the sub came blasting right out of the side of a mountain, in a great big spray of cascading bubbles.

Mr Nugent lifted his specs and began to read off the side of the carton:

> *Stingray* was the first Supermarionation series to feature marionette characters with interchangeable heads that enabled them to show a variety of expressions. The nuclear-powered machine featured on the cover of this box is the flagship of the World Aquanaut Security Patrol (WASP). It is piloted by the square-jawed Captain Troy Tempest (comes complete with posable limbs) along with Southern navigator, nicknamed 'Phones'. Their mortal enemy, as the series' many fans will know already, is Titan of Titanica.

I was still in a daze long after he had finished.

But nothing prepared me for what was coming next.

When I heard him exclaim:

—Seeing as you've brought a guest into our house, I think he ought to be given first go. What do you say, Philip? Do you think, in the circumstances, that he ought to be accorded such a privilege?

& I know that it's possible – indeed, most likely – that anyone reading this won't believe it happened.

But it did, you see – & I ought to know, because I was there.

& which is the reason it will remain forever, my most unforgettable day.

And why, even yet, I still find it hard to swallow when I look up and see him there, smiling – reflected in the lenses of his father's big brown glasses.

—Here, he says, handing me Captain Troy Tempest, and play with him for as long as you like.

—For, after all, we're not in any hurry, says his father.

As he sits in the armchair and begins to read the paper, shuffling it a little as me and Philip began walking the two-foot high commander across the carpet – with him taking the salute by the sideboard mirror.

Where Joe was busy shaking the dice for the Snakes & Ladders, and the only thing bothering me that nothing as beautiful and magnificent as this would ever again be able to happen in my life, so much so that it almost brought me to tears – and probably would have only for Philip's mother, in her apron, arrived in with a tray of steaming scones – and said, as she laughed and whipped away a teacloth:

—Ta-ra, little gentlemen! Roll up for some sconesies – because it's time, or didn't you know, for the one and only *Teatime with Tommy*!

At the very same time as the host looked up from the keys and announced that such-and-such had written in with some special request.

As off he went, like billy-o again, with his great long fingers sweeping up and down along the ivories.

Well man alive, as Da used to always say, what a day.

Teatime with Tommy.

Chapter 13

Leaves

I'm a fair while now over sixty, as Wee Pat Casey used to always say, so I reckon there's every chance that any day now I'll end up the same as The Professor, so why not take my chances and scarper? That's all I've got to say.

Because, really after all, what is the worst that can happen?

Especially since I've done my homework – so, no fucking Russians or similar mishaps this time.

I can do it – I just know I can.

& all I want to do is make sure and finish the *Yaroo* – in order to leave something substantial behind.

A sort of little memorial, you might say.

Here lies Frank – within these very pages.

Yaroo!

I met The Professor on the stairs, coming down.

—C'mere! he says, grabbing a hold of me by the sleeve, do you have any idea why it was I was put on earth?

And, even yet, I still can't properly decide what to answer.

The more my experience moves towards his – and I dread waking up in the night, seeing myself exactly like he did – wondering who are all those people moving around inside that lighted room – wondering did they ever exist, or do I imagine them?

Could it be that you imagine yourself? I often think.

Observing the drifting figures as they reach up slowly for the purpose of retrieving a book – setting a lamp down, ever so gently, on a table.

Before turning, in puzzlement, towards the pale-lit window – elevating a single fretful eyebrow.

As though to inquire:

–Do you have any idea who I might be?

Or was?

As a matter of fact – even though I'm still reluctant to admit it – only two nights ago I experienced that same professorial-type sensation again.

When, in the small hours, roundabout 3 a.m., I should think, I found myself suddenly shooting awake – and becoming aware of this unfamiliar, halting sound.

Like crackling.

With it taking me, embarrassingly, quite a number of minutes to determine precisely what its origins were – that they actually had a physical, real basis – and weren't proceeding from inside my head.

It turned out to be an electrical fault – a malfunctioning landing light.

Then I remembered that I had passed Corrigan on a stepladder underneath it earlier that day.

Obviously he hadn't made much of job of it, I thought.

Not that that came as any surprise.

As if I cared one way or another, I thought, turning on my side and allowing all the tension to flow out of me like a river.

& with the funniest thing happening then – being consumed in the process by what I can only describe as this immense sense of gratitude or something – that everything, & in spite of all my earlier and evidently quite unwarranted anxieties – had turned out to be so surprisingly ordinary.

But then, as I lay there, this renewed great big wave of sadness overwhelmed me as I thought of what I had overheard The Professor saying.

He was going over it all again in his mind – the football match from the year 1947, when he and Colleen Turley had held hands in Central Park.

–The year, he continued, when County Cavan almost conquered the world. And then, after it all was over, Colleen wanted to go to Macy's, you see. Which, in case you don't know, just happens to be one of the largest department stores. So, very well, I said – and that is exactly where we went. But I'll tell you this – I wouldn't have gone so much next or near it if I had happened to know that it was a common or garden prostitute I was dealing with. But then, I suppose, I ought to have known – when I heard her ask the assistant for a bottle of Chanel N°5, if you ever heard of that. It's a perfume. But expensive. Yes, that's where we went after the big game.

Then I remembered the way his face went – all twisted up, with his upper lip contorted in a kind of caliph-style disdain.

–Huh! he spat, I went and made a right clown of myself there, didn't I? Oh yes! Little did I know that Miss Colleen Turley – that all along she had been taking lessons in prostitution!

Then he softened a little and I heard him say:

–Ah but, sure, that's the way things go, I suppose. And, in many ways, I'll never forget Macy's. I was like a small child in my excitement when we went in the door there first, riding up and down on the escalator. Hooray for Macy's! I kept on thinking. And reflecting on now blessed and fortunate I was.

Then he went over and began tugging away at some leaves on the linden.

–Indeed, to be honest, I was on the verge of stopping complete strangers to acquaint them of my good fortune and happiness as

I sat there waiting for my future wife to complete her purchase. Such was the depth of the romantic feelings I was experiencing – for the very first time and only time in my life, in actual fact.

Pausing for a while to examine each single leaf individually, before off he went again, full throttle, loudly smacking his palm against the bark of the sturdy spreading tree.

–You see, never before had I been in such close proximity to the fairer sex. I mean, obviously, yes, I do have sisters – and one would, obviously be acquainted with the manners and habits of one's own mother. But to find myself, at the age of forty-three, working alongside such a gentle and elegant creature as my new teaching assistant, the recently appointed Miss Colleen Turley! Why, I tell you, I just couldn't believe it!

He swallowed hard and looked away. Then he hit the hollow of his left hand an almighty smack.

–Yes, absolutely from that very first day when she walked in through the waiting front door of our little country school, with her lovely little flowery briefcase and that sweet little pillbox hat & smart tweedy coat, I knew almost instantly that a new world had begun – one entirely unfamiliar to me. But also, one most welcome, I really must insist. Or so, sad to say, it seemed at the start. Are you listening to me, leaves?

Then, without warning, he suddenly turned on his heel.

–*Frogs!* he barked, that's what she started bringing into the classroom. And then, if you don't mind, wandering off to the meadows for the purpose of spotting more amphibians!

–But the frogs had just been the start of it, he continued, with this new go-ahead assistant. Now she had started introducing chemistry – with her experiments stimulating even the younger children in a manner which had to be seen to be believed.

He swished a great handkerchief out of his pocket and mopped his brow. And then got up once more and walked around.

Before deciding to sit down again.

—I mean, I did know for a fact that some of the others were jealous of her, he explained, and that certain individuals in the community wanted her out from the very minute she came in the door. They even took exception to the kind of blouses she wore!

—Yes, he continued explaining to his handful of leaves, that's what I said.

And it was after that that the letters all started.

Yes, he said, leaves. Anonymous letters from various irritated parents, explaining how they saw no reason why a woman assistant teacher in receipt of taxpayers' money should be permitted to come into work wearing tight skirts and low-necked blouses with flowers.

He began nibbling abstractedly on a leaf as he sobbed.

—Then someone else took it upon themselves to pay the bishop a personal visit.

He sank down on his knees and began to clear a space underneath the tree, commencing a frenzied motion with his fingers, scooping out great handfuls of earth.

—So then, leaves. Would you like to know what happened?

One by one he began to conceal them, covering them over with little piles of earth.

—You would? Very well then, I'll tell you. I'll tell you what happened to the lovely Colleen Turley. She ended up in Ballinasloe Mental Hospital, that's what. And would you like to know why? I didn't have the courage to stand up to them and fight for her!

His lower lip was trembling violently.

Then he stood up and appeared to lose all interest in both the scooping and his leaves.

—I was affronted, you see, by what it was she had done to me in New York City.

He rubbed his eyes.

–Affronted, yes.

And I'm sorry about that, he said, really sorry.

Before landing an extremely violent blow in the middle of nothing, with his fist.

–But, all the same, leaves, or anyone else who wants to listen, she had no business, either, doing what she did. No, no business at all – arriving, uninvited, into my room in the middle of the night and suggesting to me that we do bad things. Things that are prohibited for unmarried people to do, under the laws of God. The naughty thing. She had purchased the lace gloves specially, she said. Go back to your own room, Colleen, this instant, I had to tell her – but she gave me this smile and batted her lashes as she said to me firmly that no she wouldn't, flaunting her perfume from Macy's like a common you-know-what as she crawled between the covers, still batting away. Yes, perhaps nowadays when things have been turned upside down and everywhere you look there are prostitutes and gays and men who are women turned back from having been men, yes it may well indeed be possible. Just as, in some other world that is, unfortunately not as yet born, somehow I might have somewhere located the courage not to destroy poor Colleen the way that I did. Yes, where perhaps I might have actually possessed the courage of my convictions. Do you think that's possible, anyone? What about you – do you think so, leaves?

As he returned and began gathering them up by one, laughing away as he lined them all up on the wall.

And then began stroking the one he called Colleen Turley – assuring her that, yes, it was of course perfectly acceptable for her to come to his room that night.

–Just as it ought to have been that first time in New York. Because now it doesn't matter – you see now, I'm not afraid!

Making sure that she knew that he'd never again undermine her, not to mention side in the most cowardly fashion with the parents and the church in their campaign to undermine her.

–Oh no, said The Professor, swallowing the leaf. The one that he knew was Colleen Turley.

& who now, as a result, would always be with him.

Deep inside of him, forever, part of his soul.

Except that she wouldn't, as he well knew.

Because Colleen Turley was a woman and anyway, she was long since dead.

Just like the love they could have had that he'd rejected.

& why he was left in the rain by the linden
vomiting up leaves
that just wouldn't stay down
along with the conviction that he
wasn't to blame.

Chapter 14
Cat's Eyes Cunningham

A sad story surely, one I shall most definitely be including in the forthcoming holiday issue of *The Big Yaroo*, to which I am sure you are all looking forward.

& a copy of which I intend to leave behind for you all – for, make no mistake, this time I have no intention of returning to Fizzbag.

So it will be up to you to fully document events surrounding 'Frank's Big-Time World-Beating Smasheroo Breakout'.

And which, believe me, will have nothing to do with 'He Just Happened to Strike It Lucky' or anything else – for this time, absolutely nothing has been left to chance.

With only three full days left to go before those old *Big Yaroo*s start rolling off the presses and you'll look around …

–Frank?

But I'll be gone.

Whizz! – speeding through those old electronic gates on my bicycle.

Never to be seen again.

I've checked the codes on the gates & reckon that now I've got the times down perfect – and will definitely be making my play somewhere between 11.03 and 11.05 – just as soon as Fr Ron goes through them in his Mazda, on his way to Aunt Somebody in Carlow, who I know he's bringing out for her Easter dinner.

I guess you could say I've been shadowing him a little, and paying close attention to his conversations.

& what with him buying her flowers and eggs, I reckon he ain't gonna have this old Frank on his mind – or is going to be entertaining any tired old notions regarding bust-outs.

Pretty much pegging me for a failure in that department – and I don't blame him.

No, not one bit, for it must surely rank as one of the most ramshackle and ham-fisted attempts at liberation ever, my previous effort I mean.

But that's mainly because I hadn't bothered to do enough planning.

However, like they say, you learn from your mistakes.

With every single detail, right down to the very last second, remaining on my mind every single minute every second of every day.

And it really does make the most perfect sense – especially when you think that both my mother and father died at Easter.

As a matter of fact, everyone belonging to me is dead – I'll be including all their names in *The Big Yaroo*.

The final issue, I mean.

The Easter Sunday Special – forthcoming.

I'll be posting some issues, as well, out to Portrane.

Which, they tell me, is just about the closest thing you can get to a holiday camp – in a mental hospital, they mean.

With the only thing being that no matter what way you look at it, when your freedom is curtailed and you're incarcerated, you're spiritually ossified, circumscribed. Kind of, I don't know – snared.

Especially, as I say, when everyone you know is dead.

With you now having to get used to this new idea that if you happen to wake up in the night, all cold and sweaty, there is no one to whom you can turn to and say:

–I think I might need help.

***

Oh, you can chat with Dr Cecil, yes, and Mrs Beacon too. Of course you can – but they're not getting any younger either and as well as that they've got problems of their own.

As a matter of fact, I met Mary only just this morning, coming along the front of the house with her trusty old pet Toddy Ray lying quivering in a special transporter.

She was on her way to the cat clinic, Tiny Paws, she told me.

–How is she, I said, and what does Mary do, go and drop the box on the front step of her little cottage, all a-dither and shaky, fiddling with things.

& when I look inside what do I see only all this sputum covering a newspaper on the floor of the cat transporter, as startling as the green on the leaves on the linden.

It really was horrible, I'm sorry to have to say – and I genuinely wish there was something I could have done.

But, like I'm saying, that's one thing you learn – you see, that there's only so much you can do for anyone.

With everybody laughing away as if there's not a thing in the world that's bothering them – only then when you look around, what do you see only them sitting there, pale, tapping away at their thumbs, looking like they're about to break down.

With the *Emmerdale* theme sweeping away across the moors as they try not to think too much about the ones they loved and their many departed relatives.

So it's a hard old station.

Ever since Tom the Weaver's death, I've been thinking a lot about things like that.

& I wish I didn't.

But sometimes you have no choice.

Just like I didn't last night when it all came back, more vivid than ever – that day in Mount Argus, which I wish had never happened, for Tommy's sake mainly.

Out of respect for the dead.

Because a funeral's no place for anger and spite.

Anyone with any measure of decency knows that.

But then it wasn't me who was responsible for it happening.

I mean, if you'll excuse me, I don't remember saying:

–There goes the murderer. There's the fellow who slaughters his neighbours.

Because all I wanted was to pay my respects – say a prayer for Tommy and then go home, get back in the car.

But some people can't – just won't allow you to do that.

& I still was bitter – so that's why I saw myself standing back there in the churchyard again – as if no time had passed at all.

With all the mourners waiting around in their veils and gloves and long black coats, looking pale outside the chapel door as they waited for the bearers to emerge with Tommy's coffin.

I could sense the hostility so powerfully that it nearly made me shout out loud.

As I stood there thinking about it, in the chapel corridor – seeing that grey, taut face again, like a bloodless greyhound.

With not so much as a muscle moving in his cheeks as up went the hand and he muttered to his friend:

–Yes, that's him. That's Brady. That's the kind of fucker our Tommy had to put up with.

Small wonder we ended up here, he added.

It was like I was running on the spot – trying in my mind to get over as far as Weaver and have it out with him there and then – but not being able to move forward at all.

As his lips thinned out and his friend laughed aloud.

Part of me says I should be more sympathetic.

I mean, I knew that the man was a complete alcoholic.

Because Tommy had told me. I mean, I didn't make it up.

—He's got problems, a lotta stuff to deal with, he'd acknowledged on numerous occasions.

And I understand that – of course I do.

& in some other world, I would be glad & willing to help him.

In any way that I possibly could.

But then, at the same time, he didn't have any business interfering with and souring the complete & special relationship that had existed for so long between me and his wonderful brother.

No, I don't think so.

None absolutely.

Not to mention casting aspersions, saying various things about me in behind his cupped hand.

& another thing – so far as I am concerned, he really ought to have been more aware of just how someone like me might actually have been feeling.

In the circumstances, I mean.

& not only because my friend had just died but for the simple reason that I hadn't been exposed to very many such public occasions – and wasn't all that sure how to behave, not knowing how much things had changed – or if they had even done so at all.

I just can't tell you how apprehensive I was – being afraid that I might, in some way, show myself up.

&, as well as that, all the way over in the car I kept on imagining people saying: *that's him*.

Yes, that's him alright.

As I thought of strangers stopping to stare – completely forgetting about the hearse to exchange views and gossip.

Saying: *he's got a nerve!*

& what could have got into Tom the Weaver's mind – associating with the like of that!

I've never felt so rotten in my life.

Because I knew what he was thinking – he didn't have to say.

Every single thing he was saying, behind his hand – I mean, it didn't take a genius to figure it out.

–If I had anything to do with it, that devious bastard wouldn't be let anywhere near this church. We'll probably find out he had something to do with Tommy's death.

With the atmosphere probably best described, so far as I was concerned, as nothing short of chilling – like a massive sheet of impossibly thin glass poised on the point of disintegration at any moment.

As the priest droned on some distant planet.

Wittering away about how Tommy the Weaver had been a 'gentleman to his backbone' – and just how difficult his life had been.

For reasons best known only to God.

Charming, I thought.

& at one point even suggesting how it might have been a mistake for him ever to go to London.

What about the butterflies? I felt like asking.

But I didn't.

Being much too busy keeping an eye on his greyhound brother and what exactly he might be thinking of saying next.

Wondering what new slander he might come up with about me and all my family.

–The pigs, I heard him hiss very softly.

So that, really, to be honest, was the last straw.

Because by now I was feeling actually physically sick.

& needed something – some form of release.

Anything at all would have done – just to get out of there for a bit.

With any doubts I had about going ahead with the plan I'd been formulating soon to be got rid of when I saw his friend nodding.

& the greyhound stripping his teeth as he said:
—The electric chair'd be too good for the fucker.
I mean – what are you supposed to say?
Really fucking classy.
So in that respect I have no regrets.

***

No, none at all.

Except to say that in the aftermath of that complete fuck-up day outing to Mount Argus, didn't I find myself losing over two stone in weight.

Because, I think, I was missing Tommy mostly.

With the truth being that, no matter what useless, alcoholic, wife-beating manipulator he might have been unfortunate enough to be saddled with for a brother – Tom the Weaver and me: what we were, and always will be till the end, are true and proper blood brother compadres – the very next thing to kin.

Yes, and for all fucking time – and that's the way it's going to stay.

Which is why I carved our names in the bark of the linden.

And let someone try and take that off.

TW ♥ FB, from now until the end of days

I dug it in good and hard and deep, with the little wee blade that Tom used for cutting tobacco.

—So long, old friend, I said as I put it away – because that is what he was, and always will be to me, no matter what rotten lies or rumours his despicable brother felt the need to spread – when he wasn't lying drunk, slumped across the counter of some decrepit bar or other, or punching his unfortunate poor wife in the brains.

I pretended to ride a horse on a stick – all the way up as far as the main building.

And back then across the grass, as I whipped away at Trigger, having a laugh as I kept on thinking about a certain greyhound, stuck behind the wheel of a clown car, coming apart.

I was only joking but.

Because those days are gone – and anyhow I'm way too old.

To be bothering my head about anyone who does the dirt on me – whether alcoholic greyhounds or anyone else.

With all of that now being consigned to history – as the prospect of freedom comes slowly nosing over the hill.

I'm so excited I just can't express it.

With there now being only two more sleeps to go – & which is why I'm making these notes in the bath – to be transferred later to the pages of *The Big Yaroo*.

> Where has he gone?
> Francie Brady: Man of Mystery!
> Edgar Wallace presents: The Missing Man
> Starring Fr Ron McGivney: where in the
> Good Lord's name can FB have gone?

The best and most exciting aspect of it all, of course, is that by getting out clean I'll have managed to redeem myself at last.

After what happened the last time, I mean.

When I'd been responsible, as I say, for just about the most embarrassing disaster of an attempted breakout ever.

Small wonder that the cops they'd brought in to do the investigating had ended up having fuck-all respect.

Truth is, I wouldn't blame them.

But that senior detective – he had really got up my nose, I have to say.

Whatever were they bringing in people from Scotland for, I told him.

—I'm not from fucking Scotland! he says, what 'you talking about?

—*Whut yee talking aboot*, I says, letting out this great big hoot of a laugh.

—I'm not from fucking Scotland! he says again.

—Och yeer! I says, now dinnae lie!

They had made up all these lies in the papers – about me taking advantage of a 'defenceless widow'.

Poor Grace Courtney, they said, to have to be faced with a monster the like of that.

'The Case of the Lonely Widow', they'd written.

Plastering it all over the very front page.

& which of course was a pack of stupid lies – because all I had done was take sanctuary in her second-hand shop.

But I suppose they're always thinking it – just like Corrigan is always saying the leopard never changes his spots.

Except that one thing they forgot – I *loved* Grace Courtney.

& would never have harmed a hair on her beautiful head.

—We know you did it, says the detective from Scotland, we know you forced your way in that night.

—Because the leopard never changes his spots, interrupts the sergeant.

—For fuck's sake, sergeant, how about learning a new tune? I says.

With the simple facts being that all I had wanted was just somewhere comfortable to lay my head.

Before being satisfied that the coast was clear – and I could once and for all get the hell out of Dublin city.

Because I was already feeling foolish enough – having picked the worst night of the year, maybe the century – to stage my big, so-called fantastic liberation.

A state of affairs now never to be repeated, I thought.

As down I went to have a chat with Dr Cecil.

Who, happily, turned out to be all present and correct in his room.

He's a grand old fellow.

An extremely refined and scholarly gentleman – as well as being the *Yaroo*'s main financial backer.

–I was wondering, I said, have you a spare bow tie?

I didn't say it was for the breakout though.

–I have, he says, and then starts talking away about *The Big Yaroo* and how the Easter Special might be coming along.

& I have to say that he caught me in the right humour – I must have been talking for close on half an hour.

Dr Cecil is really into the creative arts – you ought to see the sheer volume of books he has stacked on his shelves.

Quite unbelievable!

Anyhow, to make a long story short, he agreed most enthusiastically to provide me with the requested item – in which, unfortunately, it transpired there was just the slightest little tear, barely visible at the corner of the right-hand wing.

It's really strange the effect that such a small and, on the face of it, completely inconsequential thing can sometimes have.

Because, when I noticed it first, I found myself becoming so upset and frustrated that I felt like going straight back up to the Doc's office and complaining bitterly.

I mean, I know it sounds funny now and not a little embarrassing, to tell the truth – but there were actually tears in my eyes as I stood there holding the bow tie in my hand.

Just staring at it.

It's going to be no good now! It's gone and ruined the whole fucking thing & I know now for sure that the liberation's going to be a failure, just like last time. OK then – now I'm not going! I'm not going to bother fucking trying to escape. I mean, why should I? When in spite of all your preparations and plans, everything is going against you again? Why does everything have to go all wrong?

I was in a right old state as I stood there on the stairs.

But, as I might have known, Mrs Beacon, out of nowhere, arrives to the rescue.

And by the time she was finished sewing, my red-and-white polka-dot accessory was every bit as good as new.

& I have to say that it really did feel excellent, just sitting there chatting away and talking to her, as she treadled the treadle of her Singer sewing machine in her slippers, laughing and joking about the days of her youth – and all the great times she used to have 'running about'.

& which just goes to show you, doesn't it – for there are times when you think that someone like Mary – that she couldn't, possibly, ever have been young – as if she'd been born the same age as now.

And which, of course, is profoundly stupid – and I'm sorry to admit I ever even thought it.

Anyhow, she fixed the dicky bow and that's all that matters – and when I stood in front of the mirror in her sitting room, she said if my mother could see me, she'd be proud.

–Yes, proud to call you her son, she said.

Those were her actual words.

–As bright as a button you are, she told me.

–I hope Toddy Ray gets better, I said.

& she rested her head on my shoulder for a bit.

–So do I. I'm expecting a call from Tiny Paws this evening. So, please God …

& which is why, as I'm sure you can understand, I felt close on ten feet tall as I stepped out of her little homely cottage – before slamming slap-bang into, would you believe it, guess who?

None other than the celebrated would-be film director and fashionista, as he styles himself.

Yes, Ricky The Shabs, sporting a brand-new pair of shades.

—What's with the dicky bow, man? he says, coolly removing the Polaroid specs.

—The big day's near. You got to be ready. Soon the time it's a coming, Ricks – all aboard for *The Big Yaroo*!

As off I went, high as a kite – snapping my fingers as I teased my mended dicky bow – cleanly elated as we all used to be after being to confession to the priest on a Saturday night.

When it'd be like your soul had been hosed down and scoured, with a bright pearly sun shining across all the new-growth plains.

Then who appears only Professor Muggsy Mr Brainbox III, only now what's he doing only jabbering away in Irish, so I have to pretend that I'm listening attentively.

Turning my dicky as I stand there, nodding away.

When all I'm thinking is: *Hurrah for Frank! Here he comes, the big breakout!*

& then when I look – Dr Brainbox is gone.

As in I go to the shed – once more, feverishly, to set about my labours.

Famous Flying Aces No. 4

(Ace test pilot Neville Duke recalls the gallantry of Britain's greatest night pilot)

Few boys at school between the two world wars had the opportunity to see so much of the world as did John Cunningham. Born near Croydon, John went to school at Whitgift and was brought up in the centre of a triangle formed by Croydon, Biggin Hill and Kenley aerodromes.

As soon as he left school, young John Cunningham joined De Havilland and learned to fly. He proved to be a brilliant pilot and by the time he was twenty-one he was a full-time

```
assistant pilot with his company. For his
brilliant service and dedication in battle,
'Cat's Eyes' Cunningham, as he became known,
was awarded the DSO.
```

By the time I was finished that, I was really quite tired but decided nonetheless to put the finishing touches to the feature I'd been writing on 'The First Great Escape' – just so no one would be in the dark after I'm gone.

& would be aware that I was sorry about what had happened to my two minders, most of all – who had lost their jobs, I'm afraid, as a result. Because poor old Lafferty and McGettigan, God love them – they hadn't, really, done anything wrong.

Been a bit lackadaisical, maybe, about their duties – but that was all.

Never in my wildest dreams did I think things would end up with poor old Lafferty being left without a penny. Heaven only knows what has become of them since – all I can say is I hope they got new positions.

Did you know that the detective actually hit me that night? And it wasn't the first occasion either. So why the fuck wouldn't I be glad to see the back of him, stupid Gordon fuck-ing Jackson fucker?

–*Ahm nae frae Scotland!* he kept on saying.

And maybe he wasn't, could be that was just something I'd got into my head – but, either way, I was glad to see him go.

Hitting people.

And slabbering away about 'sexual assault'.

Makes me fucking sick – even to think of him.

–Especially when it's the elderly! he says then, the birch is what I'd give the cretin.

–Oh shut up, Jackson! I remember saying then, I mean you don't half bloody go on now, do you?

With them all standing there in a ring around the room, just staring at me – not seeming to know what to do.

Not that I cared, rocking back and forth on the chair as I stared out the window.

With, at times, the things they were suggesting coming close to making me physically ill.

I mean, obviously, there were certain things I had done in the past – but Grace Courtney had nothing to do with any of that.

Although, I have to say, that in so many ways she was every bit as refined as the woman that they were referring to – the one whose life I'd, regrettably, brought to a close all those many long years ago, in my home town.

For a start, she had two grandchildren who attended private school in England.

A place called Haberdashers', she had told me, in London.

Yes, Alan and Ivor, she had said, such little chaps. Such characters!

She had framed their photo and hung it up in her shop – wearing their navy school blazers, grey socks and crested caps.

High-polished brown shoes.

–They are my pride and joy, I remember her saying, the reason I bother to get up in the morning. Because I lost my husband many years ago, you see – in an accident.

I could have listened to Grace Courtney for ages.

& do harm to her?

I'll break that idiot Scotsman's neck.

But there isn't any point in allowing yourself to get excited – because, in just a little over two days, the big occasion we've been waiting for will have arrived.

& I'll be out that gate like good old Steve McQueen.
Like Cat's Eyes Cunningham DSO – I swear!
I mean – is it any wonder that good old Frank, he would sing his heart out?
I don't think so!

Easter bunny
Looking funny
With his basket of eggs

I say there, Cat's Eyes – look out, old chap! Bally squadron of dastardly Jerries on the wing, by Jove!

Bells are ringing
Children singing,
'Hooray for Easter Day!'

Chapter 15
The Angel of Dresden

In my celebrated column in *The Big Yaroo* – 'The Twenty Greatest Psychiatrists of all Time!' – I will not be including Cecil's predecessor.

Mainly, I'm sorry to have to say, because Dr Kiernan was useless, the worsest pile of rubbish ever that there was in psychiatry.

& so insecure in his profession, if you ask me, that he couldn't so much as open his mouth without starting to use big words and recite never-ending paragraphs out of manuals – and then looking at you as if to say: you have to admit, I tripped you up there!

With the unfortunate truth being Clocker Kiernan knew nothing – or the next thing to it.

Certainly as regards people's 'motivation'.

Such a load of nonsense as you never heard!

–It mightn't be appropriate for a man in my position to say it – but I'm afraid, in this case, the evidence is staring us right in the face, officer.

To his credit, I have to say, the junior officer concerned said nothing.

And I'll tell you this – as soon as he said that, Clocker Kiernan was lucky that he didn't get a wallop of a chair across the head.

Because – I've said it before and I'll say it again – I wouldn't have laid a finger on the head of the lovely Grace.

Because – and I'm tired saying it – she was a lady, and more than anything, she had looked after me.

I admired her so much.

May've even loved her.

But not in a distasteful, Readers' Wives kind of way.

More like my mother.

I'll never forget that first day in Gardiner Street.

When the three of us had been supposed to go to the zoo.

Me, Lafferty and Vinnie McGettigan.

But, instead, going into a pub called The Honey Pot.

A right old dive – but my minders reckoned we'd be safe in there.

They used to ask me to go down to the bookies and place their bets while they were doing their drinking.

& that was how I first came to see her.

I was coming past the shop, checking the dockets when – what can I say?

I had just looked up.

There was a song that was playing on a transistor in the window – my mother used to sing it.

By Doris Day.

'Que Sera Sera', it was called.

It was just coming drifting out through the window – almost as though to welcome me in.

Whatever will be, will be.

That's what they mean, the words of the song.

And it was then I saw her. She was holding a little statue, carefully examining it, in her hands.

I noticed they were meticulously manicured.

I didn't have to wait.

I couldn't have anyway, even if I wanted it.

&, almost by magic, I was in.

–How much is it? I heard myself ask.

It was a pink-and-white German shepherdess, with a spotted white apron and a lovely little bonnet, made out of Dresden china.

–Do you like it? she asked.

Those were the first words I ever heard her speak.

She didn't dress like other old ladies.

Not like your mother, I mean.

That is to say she didn't wear a pinny or furry old boots, the like of what people in the sixties might have done.

But these brightly coloured loose-leg linen trousers that looked like they'd all been splashed in paint, & with a long twining pigtail that reached all the way down to her waist.

She'd been running the charity shop for two years, she said.

—But this is a funny sort of area, she said, a bit dodgy, & we've been encountering one or two problems – petty theft, etc.

—There have been a number of break-ins, she added.

But then we went back to the subject of the statue.

—If you like it, I could maybe let you have it for three or four pounds.

I was so excited by the prospect of owning it that I went and made a bollocks of myself by dropping it.

But, miraculously, it had landed, unbroken, on the carpet.

So that was my very first visit to Grace's charity shop in Gardiner Street.

& as I'm sure you can imagine – how I came to look forward to all those so-called trips to the zoo.

Which we were allowed to visit on special occasions, as a reward for extremely good behaviour.

& she said she was pleased when she heard I was working up in Cabra – in the sheltered educational scheme they have up there.

I'd read all about it on the net.

—They teach you drawing in the special school, I said.

& you should have seen what she drew for me then – the most beautiful vase of flowers.

—I like to work in charcoal, she said.

—Did you ever hear of *The Turf Cutter's Donkey*? I asked her.
An old girlfriend of mine used to love the drawings in that.

& sure enough, she told me she had.

—Patricia Lynch is probably one of my favourites, she said.

And told me to feel free to wander around the premises.

It had been a long time since I'd felt so comfortable.

With anyone.

Because the great thing about Grace was — somehow she just
knew when to leave you alone.

& carry on about her own business, doing her art or fixing
things up at the back of the shop.

She used to live in the basement, she told me.

But in recent times, it has become a little dangerous. I mean, it's
hard to believe — but second-hand clothes has become big business.

—Especially with the Eastern Europeans, she said.

—Don't talk to me about Russians! I laughed, no thanks!

& when she asked: oh why, why's that?

I just shook my head and then waved it away.

& said thanks very much, I have to get back to the school in
Cabra.

—Very well, she said, do call again. Because I really do enjoy
our little chats.

So there you are — it would be a long time before you'd hear
it, the like of that here in tired old Fizzbag,

Not in that kind of genuine, really warm way.

& it did my heart good.

& explains why, I suppose, I had got so uncomfortable the
next time when she started, asking me all these questions about
my instructors.

Not that she was launching any big major investigation or
anything. Not at all — she just wanted to know.

So, to put her at her ease, I gave her a couple of names.

Just ones I made up – I forget them now.

&, after that, we went on to something else.

Although I have to admit that, for a while, I had been a bit tense. Becoming all hot under the collar and looking around this way and that, the way I always do when I'm under pressure.

Even when I know the questions are innocent.

But with it all going well for the next two or three times – until the episode with that bastard Mickser.

I knew from the start that that was his name, having heard them use it out the front of The Honey Pot.

'Gaugers' they call them – or used to, long ago. Or sometimes 'gurriers'.

I don't know what you'd call them now.

With the big difference these days that they're all, all the time, out of their heads on this and that kind of junk, who knows or cares the fuck.

Anyhow, Mickser – his eye had been on me.

Probably right from the very start – when I'd first started showing up around the general Gardiner Street area.

Unlike in the old times, when denim jackets and iron boots would have been all the rage, now they wore hoodies and baggy old tracksuit bottoms.

–*Scumbag*! was the first thing they'd shouted.

& then, after that:

–*Rehab prick!*

I'm sorry but I couldn't allow that, I said.

They had even started to mimic my walk – with one leg lifted high above the other, moving real slow like a stepping pony.

& which was probably on account of the particular medication I was on.

Maybe if things had worked out different, we might in the end have knocked a good laugh out of it.

I'm sorry to say that they didn't, however.

With it all coming to a head this day when I'm arriving back from the bookies – there were only two of them present on this occasion, lurking in behind the galvanised fence.

–Hey you there, you rehab fuck! says Mickser. He couldn't have been more than twenty years of age. So I felt kind of bad when I thought about what was going to happen – because, like us all, I've been that age myself.

But there you go.

With them being so self-satisfied that when they were finished, they didn't notice me doubling back around by the side of the car park.

And standing behind them for well over a minute.

–Hi, I said, not even bothering to raise my voice.

Nunie was the other one. Nunie – I mean, what a fucking name.

Anyway, soon as he seen me – he took off and legged it back into the flats.

I slipped the knife out of my jacket and just let it rest there, folded in my hand.

At first Mickser seemed to think it was a great old joke.

–*Oh*! he says.

Oh, if you don't mind.

& then starts explaining how it had been Nunie who'd done the bulk of the shouting.

–You done nothing, I said, and he laughs.

–Nunie's a bleeding headcase, he says, looper man.

–Looper, I said, looper man.

–Yeah! Everyone knows that.

–I didn't know it, I said, with a bit of a smile, but then of course I'm not from anywhere around here. I'm just a visitor.

–Just a visitor, are you man? he says, that's cool.

—Yes it is, I agreed, it is for sure.

As he moves to go and I say:

—Oh don't. Please stay.

With him starting to stammer some stupid excuse.

—Oh! Late for an important appointment, are you? I said.

With the blood beginning to drain from his face when I touched the poor bastard on the earlobe with the edge of the blade.

—Do you like jam? I asked him then.

—What? he says.

—What do you mean 'what'? I said. Jam — do you like it?

—I don't know, he says, I don't often get it much.

—Do you not? I said, and just nicked him a little with the point of the smaller knife — the one you pulled out, that was used for cutting tobacco.

—Jesus, man! he screamed. & you want to see him.

Such a baby.

—You should have seen me that day in Newtown. Mammy, God help her — she thought the Loch Ness monster must have arrived at the door!

—What? he says, as I nicked him again.

Then I said:

—Get away to fuck. Get on out of here, and fast. & don't ever fucking bother me again!

But I had to laugh when I said about the jam.

Wherever the fuck that had come out of.

***

Never in my life have I seen such a dump — as Gardiner Street, I mean. I sometimes wonder is it a street at all, or just a place where the likes of poor old Mickser go to drink cans and pump themselves up till they're out of their heads on smack.

So, in a way, to be honest, I don't really hold it against them – knowing if I'd grown up in a place like that, most likely I'd have ended up the very exact same – surrounded by syringes & prostitutes & rats.

–Ah, there you are! shouts Vinny when I came in, we were wondering where it was you had got to!

& to make matters even better, the two of them ended up with winners at the 3.35 in Newmarket.

So everyone was happy in the van, going home.

As I did my best to put Mickser out of my mind.

Thinking to myself that if he was in one of the gangs that were roaming around, stealing things and terrorising innocent people like Grace Courtney, who were only trying to make an honest living, then he had better fucking watch out.

But I didn't think he was.

We weren't long back when I ran into The Professor – with the pair of us wandering off to enjoy a stroll.

–I've never, in my life, been in better form, says he.

But I'm sorry to have to say that I wasn't listening to a word he was saying. Being far too busy thinking about introducing Grace to Tom the Weaver – with the pair of them chatting, like I knew they would – about butterflies and freedom.

& then moving on to discuss art and music and films.

It made me feel a hundred per cent, thinking that – knowing now that I was included.

You see, I've never really had a girlfriend – not a proper one anyhow.

One, I mean, that you could be romantic with – like Carole King, maybe, or perhaps Sandy Denny.

Tommy had always been fond of playing those songs: Your eyes are like the waves of the sea, diamond blue they shine, & all this.

& which is why it was always going to upset me – how could it not? – if anyone implied that the way I was attracted to Grace Courtney was the same as these letters you often see in what used to be called off-colour magazines of the *Fiesta* type. You know what I mean?

Because nothing could be further from the truth.

Believe it or not.

But my head was hurting thinking all these things. So I put the little china princess up on the sill and just sat there thinking about how well things had all worked out.

& how, for the first time, in what had to be years – I had actually begun to feel hope again.

& you'll never guess what I went and did then.

Said a prayer to that little Dresden angel – the very same way I used to, to Our Lady.

It really was wonderful.

The best feeling I've had for years.

& which is why I'll be bringing her out the gate – snugly tucked down into my pannier bags.

–For she is gonna go nowhere without me! I remember saying as I rose up off my knees.

Nearly letting out the biggest yaroo of all – right from the very pit of my stomach.

Now, thank heaven, we're almost there.

Roll on The Great Escape!

Dickie Attenborough – eat your heart out!

But, for me, it's time to roll up the sleeves and make this old Easter Special the envy of publishers all across the world – even motherfucking J. Jonah Jameson, cigar-chomping nemesis of much put-upon Peter Parker.

(Aka Spider-Man – of Forest Hills, Queens, New York City, of course!)

'Tonight in Tokyo'
(A *Big Yaroo* travel special)

The light was already declining as I remained
there, tentatively, in the wavering shadows
of the wharf and the promise of tropical
sundowns yet to come — among the cargo
boats, sampans, tramps and junks. Only
then becoming aware, as plucked strings
and a bamboo flute, temporarily erased by
the majestic reverberations of a ceremonial
gong, echoed somewhere close by, that my
Singhalese guide had already departed — as
I turned, standing above the oily, lapping
water — and saw, to my amazement — just as
had been promised in the dream, obscured
behind a pearl-grey curtain of cloud, the
unmistakable City of Once.

Before slowly realising that those shockingly familiar streets
that were now laid out in front of me were deserted in a way that
I'd never before remembered – long grey timid stretches of grime
pierced with square holes that made windows as I picked my way
through the deserted laneways of descending dusk.

There seemed to be no movement of any kind whatsoever.
We had lived in the house with the green door, with the rhythm
of our lives, the very same as that of our neighbours, continuing for years without any interruption – tragically, until recent
days. & oh what pleasant times they had been, I recalled. With
'Tonight in Tokyo' by Sandie Shaw drifting from a transistor on
a windowsill somewhere nearby, evoking an orient with flotillas
of junks and web-sailed sampans, far from the rolling hillocks
to which the last straggles of suburbia gave way, here in the little

town where I had first seen the light of day. & where I had suc-
cumbed to the fresh, invigorating perfumes of the healthy ozone,
in this place where happy, giddy families had once enjoyed their
picnics in the summer. And where somewhere close by I could
hear a snatched phrase of the theme from *Housewives' Choice* lilting from what seemed an almost military arrangement of raised
sash windows. Look! There's a woman shaking a rug with her
hair in plastic curlers – here in this fresh new spring of hire-pur-
chase TV sets, washing machines whirring and spruce orchestras
rendering popular themes. As the last tiny woman in a back
garden hung up a shirt – in this city, this domain of scullery,
kitchen & back alleys black as pitch, with one cold water tap
dripping in a concrete yard & a tin bath hanging behind every
coalhouse door. Inside each house there would be serviettes and
doilies – and, covering the table, a lime-green, velvet tablecloth.
Where shadows down on their knees sang the very same songs
they had crooned to first infants, all the while busy waxing lino
in hallways and still, hushed sitting rooms where three-panelled
mirrors on chains hung over green-tiled fireplaces whose shade
echoed that of the tablecloth. Where you could smell coal and
lavender polish, and overhear whispers, seemingly amplified,
from dark sculleries. Voices I knew mimicking the rhythm of
the slow-ticking clock – as hands, thin and plump, rose upwards
to carefully cover their mouths as they uttered my name – and a
squat, jerking robin alighted on the garden wall, monitoring all
of the subdued activity with eyes that were shockingly fierce &
alert. Instinctively recording conversations, which might have
come from the time when my grandmother, in her floral pinny
& furry zipped boots, had turned the handle of her wooden
mangle, squinting towards the sun beneath a flurry of mad-
dened white sheets.

But now it seemed as though no one lived, or indeed had ever had done so, behind this privet hedge or that high picket fence, in any one of the many reach-me-down dolls' houses.

Where thin kitchen curtains fell to three inches of the sill, as tables were cleared and readied once more.

I made my way past the overflowing bins, avoiding the spillage of soggy eggshells and rotted cabbage stalks. Then I heard my name being called – from far away across the slated wet roofs of the town.

–Welcome to the Beautiful City of Once! they cried, & I looked up and saw all my old pals coming running towards me, with cat's-vane marbles rattling loudly in their pockets.

–Hooray for you coming! I heard one of them trill gleefully, we thought that maybe there was a chance you wouldn't.

–Because no one we knew ever bothers to come here any more here to the beautiful City of Was.

Then I looked up and saw Wee Pat Casey wandering up and down with his cap turning in his hand.

I've never seen him look so alone.

–Pat! I called out, hey there Pat!

But he didn't seem to hear me.

Then he sat under a tree and commenced sobbing fitfully.

–I remember it too, I could hear him say, all the snow that fell that day & me poor auld mumbly wee wife Trixie-Mae, her a-rambling with the doggie out in the fields among the drills. & now I've been searching for her everywhere, so I have, and sight nor sign can I find of her – here in what they tell you is the most beautiful City of Ever! But is it – is it really, I ask you – or is all of that just a lie as well? & the beautiful city that is supposed to be Once – maybe, long ago, it's been lost too. Oh God, oh no! Please tell me it's not true!

As my two pals bent down and, with the sharp end of a stone, began scoring a distended oval shape in the clay.

Marbles then were all the rage.

Marbles played, sometimes, with taws.

Taws, if you ever heard of – or remember them.

Taws, that's right.

Taws, yes.

Perhaps best described as an uncommonly large & transparent sphere of glass the size of the average plum or extra-large gooseberry – snugly perched, on the slope of your thumb.

You could still hear *Housewives' Choice* undulating through the open window.

As we looked up to see Fr Dominic approach.

& who extended his arm, slowly began opening his fist, as he said:

–What do you think it might be, I wonder – what's in here I mean? What I have here in my fist?

–It's a taw, one of the boys suggested, I think perhaps it might be a taw, Father.

The priest said nothing – just stood there, smiling faintly.

As Wee Pat Casey stood up and began roaring incoherently, not unlike someone having a fit.

–Leave them alone! Can't you see they're only children & don't belong in this city of fucking phantasms – for that's all it is!

Through the half-open window, *Housewives' Choice* was beginning all over again.

In the hollow of the priest's open hand rested an eye, a human one – viscous, vividly veined.

–I think you know the origin of this, he said, turning specifically to me and ignoring the others completely.

My face burned as I looked away in shame.

When we looked again, Father Dominic was gone.

As was the City of Never Would Be Again, and all of us knew who was to blame for that.

Chapter 16

Terminal

Now there's just a little over a day and a half left, I have to set about getting all the rest of my things ready – and, what with the amount I have to do, don't have much choice but to leave some of my best articles unfinished.

Such as, for example, an item I'd been planning on the worst police interview ever to be held, whether in the history of Scotland Yard or anywhere else.

Mostly starring that haggis-munching idiot, Windsor Davies with the moustache.

Boy, did he like to make your life a misery.

–Don't tell me lies – you had it all planned from the very beginning, breaking into that defenceless woman's basement.

–After all, he adds, it's not the first time you did it, is it.

–Well, as a matter of fact, in case you don't know, it is – because they don't have basements in the town where I was born, I said.

Because it's in cities, mostly, that you get them.

–Not that I have to go around explaining myself to the likes of you, Windsor, I said, so how about maybe you go to hell?

–My name's not Windsor, he says, and gives me a wallop. &, like I told you before – I don't even come from Scotland.

–Oh do you not? says I, well God help anywhere that you do. Come from, I mean.

& you could see Clocker Kiernan going red in the face.

Like he's thinking that you're doing it again – bringing the hospital into bad repute.

But to be perfectly honest, I was way past caring.

& all I could think was – I hope that Grace doesn't hold it against me.

Because I wasn't sure.

I mean, after all – I had told her lies. About the sheltered workshop up in Cabra, etc., etc.

–But what's done is done, I said to Kiernan, and he looks at me like a turkey that's swallowed a golf ball – the spit of Charles Hawtrey, if you ever happened to hear of him, from the *Carry On* flicks that often come on in the middle of the day.

–I can't believe it, he says, after everything I've done for you.

–I'm sorry Hawtrey, I mean Doc, I said.

& I was.

At least until he started agreeing with Scotty Davies and all of the other detectives who started getting every bit as bad.

With all this let's just finish it here and now and do everyone a favour – kick the fucker out the window.

But, fortunately, they didn't – and in the end just got tired and sent me back to my room with a minder. Whose name I don't know but he sure was some size.

You're fond of the burgers & chips, I said.

But I don't think he heard me.

I had plenty of time to think in my room after that.

About the night of the break-in long ago and how I'd gone and got it all arseways with the so-called Russians. Who had turned out not to be Russians at all.

Which shows just how much I know about foreigners.

I suppose because there weren't that many when I was growing up – not in Ireland at least.

& certainly not in our little town.

—Here now, wait a minute! maybe I should have said, I thought it was me who was supposed to be breaking in!

& there definitely was a funny side to it, with the three of them built like fucking brick shit houses, and in no hurry to walk away from someone who was muscling in on their territory.

They were a professional second-hand-clothes-robbing gang, you see, who did this for a living.

& it was just my luck to walk right into their arms, when I should have been miles from anywhere, with no one having the faintest idea.

Just where Frank the famous escaper had gone!

With the sad truth being that, Twin Towers or no Twin Towers, I'd probably have been safer in downtown Manhattan.

Would you like to know something about foreign women? They're just as bad as the men so they are.

—Let me at him! and scrunch with the heel.

Ah yes, they were wild old times. With me one minute chatting away with Grace and the next a pile of mush lying underneath a mound of second-hand clothes, with every bastard in Europe tramping on top of me.

She had been everywhere that you could think of in the world – during the Summer of Love. Her real, actual name was De Courcey-Meers (she'd changed it later on) – and she'd been born and reared in a place called De Courcey Hall.

—But what, may I ask, is it that takes you to this dump? I asked her.

I did in me eyeball.

—Why did you set up this business? I said.

—To help others less fortunate than me in the world, she explained.

& I have to say I was pleased to hear that – feeling that, in some small way, I was part of it.

I nearly wet myself when she said she had been at Blackbushe.

& I started blathering away about Bob Dylan & Graham Parker & The Rumour, the very same as if I'd been there myself.

With me knowing, of course, all there was to know about these concerts and things, thanks to all the time that I'd spent with Tommy the Weaver.

We were in the middle of that chat when I looked up and seen one of her best friends coming in, & who, although she was nice, wouldn't have been able to hold a candle to Miss Grace, not a chance.

As a matter of fact, somewhat to my surprise, I found myself thinking her a little bit common.

Of the type that might have been Mickser's ma.

But no way was I going to hold it against her.

As off she went, yammering on about some community programme she was on.

–This is Eugene Flood, Grace told her, and for a minute I nearly said no I'm not, going and forgetting all about the fact that that was what I had told her, myself.

–He's been showing me some of his artwork – I'll have to give you some. And one day he hopes to publish a magazine.

–That's my ambition, I said, going red.

But I don't think she was listening.

After I came home that day, I put the angel at the bottom of my drawer, all safely wrapped in a coat of soft purple tissue.

In a way I felt guilty, as though she'd taken the place of Our Lady.

But with the great thing being, once I explained the situation, you could see straight away that Our Lady did understand.

As I stood there in the rain, all stuttery and awkward, and heard her say – the very same as before:

–Did you think I expected you to stay a child forever, Francie?

& I could have leapt twenty feet in the air, the very second I heard her saying that.

As off I went, with a whole new world of wonder, it seemed to me, beginning to open up all over again.

Leading me to getting out my coloured pencils and starting to sketch all these pictures in rainbow colours – and putting little stories from the old days along with them, assorted memories from a time when it had all made sense.

Memories such as this, which was the first one I ever wrote – and which had led me, ultimately, I suppose, to publishing my very own periodical.

The Q Bikes

Three young cyclists from the district of Carn have formed a junior flying squad to help people in trouble. The citizens of their home town have presented the Q Bikes with a brand-new bicycle each in recognition of their brave deeds.

Q3 Joseph Purcell, residing at No. 4, The Square.

Q2 Philip Nugent, residing at No. 2, The Diamond.

Q1 Frank 'Francie' Brady, residing at No. 7, The Terrace.

Below is a picture of the model presented to each of the boys at a specially convened meeting in the town square this summer — a memorable occasion for all concerned.

Explorer Model 58, for boys only — with a sturdy eighteen-inch frame and curved top tube, twenty-six-inch wheels, Dunlop tyres, caliper brakes, 'All-Rounder' handlebar. In Sunset Yellow with Sky Blue details. Single speed £18 12s. 6d. or 3-speed with 'Twist Grip' control £21 4s. 10d.

On the Trail of the Umbrella Men

The Q team met in the disused shed at the back of the railway, which acted as their temporary HQ, before the hut they were building for that express purpose was completed.

Q3, Joseph Purcell, was on hand to announce the specifics of their intended mission.

The Umbrella Men

Membership: an unspecified set of numbered members: Numbers 4 and 17 identified.

Purpose: to rob for profit.

Enemies: Francis Brady, Joseph Purcell, Philip Nugent.

Base of Operations: a deserted mansion house on the outskirts of the town of Carn, Ireland.

History: the Umbrella Men are a gang of thieves who dress in business suits and bowler hats and use jet-propelled umbrellas to fly and commit robberies. The handle can be extended to allow the Umbrella Men to ride it like a stirrup. The umbrellas also include a motorised tip blade that can cut through steel like butter. Knockout gas can be projected out of the handle.

'Every ounce of courage you possess will be called on for this mission, team,' said Joe, 'so all I have got to say is – good luck to you all, and may God be with us – who are forever the Q Assembly!'

&, after having written that – no matter how I tried, I couldn't stop thinking about bikes and missions illustrating strip after gaudy strip of me coming – *blam!* – bursting out through the gates on various up-to-the-minute types of cycles – with these little inch-high figures, who turned out to be Ronnie and Professor Big Brains, running after me waving their fists furiously as they screeched & bawled:

–*Get back here you! Come back! Come back!*

So, in a way, before I ever went near the office, I already had the makings of a magazine completed – even if I didn't use all that much of it.

I had boxes and boxes of drawings, so I had.

With it, as I say, perhaps being inevitable I should end up as Fizzbag's answer to J. Jonah Jameson, *The Big Yaroo*'s editor-in-chief, preparing for what promises to be the greatest vamooso in all of prison history.

Which is why I've drawn a little picture of herself, Our Lady, to feature on the inside front page – with me at the top right-hand corner, smiling all delighted and giving her the thumbs up.

She looks so good – with The Atom standing facing her, on the other side, in the exact same metallic blue colours.

All the things you can come up with in comics.

Anyway, they said I had to stay in solitary for a month, and after that I was, more or less, a completely broken man.

& all I can say is, that I'm afraid if you believe that, then I am extremely worried for your mental health – with the actual truth being that, just as soon as they opened that door, I was off away out the front like a bullet – and looking everywhere for Professor Muggs the Big.

–Yes, Mr Big Brains, wherefore art thou gone? I kept on repeating to myself as I scoured the grounds.

& who I ran to earth about fifteen minutes later – in the middle of a crossword puzzle, all curled up in behind a tree.

& who, as soon as he seen me, rolled *The Irish Times* up into a ball and flung it away, throwing his arm around me as he laughed:

–Why, there you are, Frank – just in time for tea, as it happens. So, let us perambulate in the general direction of the refectory!

–Yes indeed, Professor my man – where they are serving our favourite Tyrone bangers!

–As we march once more in search of the Cookstown sizzle!

Which reminded me of poor old Vinnie, God love him – cooking bangers and chips in the back of the van, full-drunk after the pub, on this little Primus stove that he had.

With my other supposed minder, Lafferty – blue in the face from smoking dope.

I mean – can you believe it?

I wonder what Kiernan might have said about that.

It's just a pity that it ended the way it did – for I had enjoyed those old cooking sessions, especially if one of the boys had come good at the races.

–Aye aye! Just can't bate the auld Cookstown sizzle! I remember Vinnie used to say.

As Lafferty fell back with his legs splayed in the air.

A Day at the Zoo by Frank M. Brady
Once upon a time we all went to the zoo in Dublin city, which they says is one of the finest enclosures in Europe.

Except, sad to say, we didn't go at all.
The End

But zoo or no zoo, they definitely were some good old days – especially that Saturday when Vinnie McGettigan leaned over, and said:

–We were thinking of having one last pint – what do you say? Maybe you'd go down and place us a few more bets? There's a fiver in it, Frank …

& to which I responded:

–Oh, absolutely not. In fact, I am sorry but I take grave offence. Because that is not what you're supposed to be here to do.

Like fuck I did – as I grabbed the money out of his hand and tore off down to the bookies on the corner.

& nearly pissed my trousers when I seen it, just the very same as it was when I was a child – with the same little nautical suit and cap and his two legs parted as he looked at me out the window. & the hairs, I swear, rising up stiff as briars on the back of my neck.

'Captain Troy Tempest' Grace had printed on a neat little label.

He even had the very same boots and badge – with the trademark insignia W.A.S.P. (World Aquanaut Security Patrol) pinned to the middle of his security-style vest.

I was so taken aback that perspiration began streaming down my forehead.

As I stood there, frozen, with the money clenched in my fist.

& I'll tell you this now, straight up and honest, not so much as a word of a lie – I couldn't have stopped myself if I'd tried.

–*I have to have it*! I cried as I went in, and I know that Grace must have been taken aback, don't sell it to anyone else. Because if I haven't enough dosh, I know I'll get it somewhere!

–Stand by for action, Marineville! Anything can happen in the next half hour!

Those were the words spoken every Sunday evening at 5.30 pm by the nautical marine commander concerned – sworn enemy of Titan, tyrannical ruler of Titanica and commander of a brutal warrior race called the Aquaphibians.

Captain Troy was in love with Titan's slave, Marina – a mute young woman from the undersea city of Pacifica who could breathe underwater – and had sworn, many times, to rescue the beautiful maiden from his evil clutches.

I hadn't seen him since that evening in Philip's – when we'd been busy watching *Teatime* with you-know-who.

But there he was, which was why such a great big lump began to swell in my throat – as I remained there, transfixed, by that very same protruding lip and poseable arms.

–I wouldn't dream of letting it go to anyone else, I remember Grace Courtney saying as she wrapped it up, and I almost felt like embracing her on the spot.

& no, not like you see in Readers' Wives or any of that – the way Windsor Davies had implied in his interview.

No – because, you see, it was much simpler than that.

–Yes, thank you Mammy – and then just a kiss.

Or a gooser, as my own mother used to call it – before throwing herself off the old wooden bridge and remaining for three days with the rats before they discovered her.

So what could be wrong with that?

Beats me, Windsor Davies.

But I didn't care – because now I had Troy Tempest *and* an angel! Fun times in Frankietown – that, I'm afraid, is all that I can say.

As in he popped to my ever-growing pannier of accoutrements – in preparation for our mass departure!

Talking about pannier bags & accoutrements, I am sure you are wondering just what it is I think I am doing with all these coins I am carefully arranging inside a tin box along with Queen Dresden and the incomparable Captain Tempest.

Well, the answer to that, like so much in life – you live, you die and all your relatives go before you ha ha – is really quite simple – I've been collecting them assiduously on eBay now for months.

But, Jesus Mary fuck – I keep on dropping them!

Only two more sleeps to go – can you believe it?

I'm nervous as a kitten, I really am, I swear to God, even just thinking about it.

Look at all these coins – so many!

The numismatist, you see, is what our Da used to call himself – in the early days when himself and Ma got married first.

–I'm going to be the best numismatist in the town, he used to say.

& I'll bet you won't guess what his wife replied to that?

Very well, then, I'll tell you.

–You already are, she used to say.

Now isn't that something?

You'd never have believed that that might be true.

But it is, you see – and no believe it or not about it.

He even had a folder with all these plastic pockets in which you could display 'to their best advantage' as he used to call it – all lined up in neat parallel rows.

Coin Monthly was the one he used to subscribe to.

Ah yes, coins.

They truly are hard to beat, you have to admit.

Thruppence.

3d.

And, as I say, ye olde farthing.

With the image of a little wren thrusting its beak up, waddling.

And the florin, too – I wonder might you possibly remember that?

That would have been to the value of two old shillings.

There's a fish on it – a leaping salmon, as a matter of fact.

It's good too – in coin terms, the 'Tops of the Town'.

But my favourite of all, when push comes to shove, would have to be:

'The 6d. Tanner'.

Because it reminds me of my poor dead uncle – the one that I told you all about earlier on.

Yes, poor old Alo, who passed away in a nursing home in Croydon.

& every time I think of that old rusted silver sixpence, it takes me back to that day long ago in the sixties when he gave me one – having arrived on the bus all the way from London, proud as punch in his raincoat, striding all the way down Main Street, with his furled umbrella tucked underneath his arm.

What a gentleman Uncle Aloysius looks – in his neat-cut suit with its red pocket handkerchief, the envy of all the men who ever worked under him in Camden.

–*Coins of the world!* he always used to say.

As I shove all my other bits of gear into my famous accoutrements pannier bags – including some very rare stamps indeed, and one extremely difficult-to-find football card – of the two Blanchflowers, would you believe.

In memory, I suppose, of Da more than anything – because I have to say that he really did like Tottenham Hotspur.

As do I – which just shows you how alike he and I have become over the years.

With there being times, as a result of that, when I feel like abandoning the whole operation – yes, downing tools on the magazine, the forthcoming escape – everything.

& I probably would have, earlier on – only for Ron happened to drop by unexpectedly and managed to knock a bit of sense into me.

–It's all planned out. You become your father, that's the way it is. So what's the point in you doing anything. Come to that, what is the point in being born at all?

—Arrah here, Frank, don't be talking like that! he says in that calm and measured way that he has – the very exact opposite of Thistlehead Davies.

& left me in such a state of good humour that I began typing like my life depended on it, and wrote what I think is probably the best story ever about a circus – at least by me.

& leaving me then as happy as Larry, not so much worried about a thing – until I looked out the window and caught a glimpse of Corrigan scuttling past, laughing to himself and swearing as he referred to me by name.

He didn't think I seen him – but I did.

—Listen, our Frank, Da says to me this evening out of the blue, when the two of us were sitting in the kitchen as usual in what he used to describe as our own private 'city of sound' – by which he meant, giving our undivided attention to the wireless.

'A Day at the Circus'
By the Editor

Yes, it was a fine old day in the middle of the sixties and Da was sitting in the armchair listening to the wireless and Ma had gone up the town to do the shopping. The sun was over in the corner looking in when all of a sudden Da spoke and said:

—*Tay!*

I'd love a cup of tea is what he meant so off with me to the kitchen to make it. It was a grand old day. Then when we were drinking it what did our Da do only say:

—To hell with England, them and their auld approvals. Sure what do you and me care about the likes of Winston Churchhill, Francie?

& I said that yes I had to agree.

Even though I was surprised he had managed it.

However, sometimes Da would drink whiskey on the quiet –
and then he could maybe say all sorts of things.

But I wasn't complaining.

Because I liked him saying it.

Signalling the end of the approvals and all.

Yes, every old row there ever was about approvals.

I mean – who cared?

Then – *plok*! – he popped open a bottle of Guinness.

Before groaning, just a little, with his eyes happy – squinting, in a way you rarely noticed but were overjoyed whenever
you did.

–It's OK now – forever, young Frank.

Then he put on his W.C. Fields voice.

–I once spent a year in Philadelphia, he said. I think it was a
Sunday!

Before standing up and speaking right into the bottle.

–Welcome to *The Wireless Show*! he beamed, starring me and
my best boy Frank!

Now he looked famous in his brown baggy suit, as off he
went, still clutching the Guinness bottle-microphone.

–As we present, for your pleasure, a special edition of our
popular weekly programme – *Numismatology Corner*. Tonight on
the show we'll be looking at the George V crown.

He produced this magnificent magnifying glass.

–Get over here, Frank, and have yourself a look at these!
Man, what a trove!

Do you know how many copper Edwardian pennies my
father had in his possession at any one time? Approaching 161. I
know that for a fact, because we counted them all together: 161.
That was our final total.

–These are going to make us rich some day, he says then, you
have no idea just how much they are going to be worth, young Frank.

146

–Squads of coppers, I says, our Da. You and me are going to be minted!

–We sure are, son, we sure are! he says, and gathers them up.

–I'll see they're left in a place that's secure. For you can't be too careful.

–That's right! I agreed, you can't be too careful these days, our Da.

& that was good, as far as it goes – but then what went and happened that you wouldn't believe – the big bag of coins, didn't it go and completely disappear!

Yes, vanish without any trace at all – almost as if the whole entire episode had been imagined.

Can you believe it?

Yes, astonishingly, the coins had somehow mysteriously taken a walk from the alleged security of their secret hiding place at the bottom of the wardrobe under a pile of old *Daily Express*es – in a cardboard OMO box expressly requisitioned for the purpose.

And now what's happened – they've all gone and done a bunk.

Hmm, looks like a job for Edgar Wallace, I remember thinking. *The Numismatology Mystery!*

So that was the state of affairs on that particular afternoon – subsequent to which the attention of your famous editor was dramatically diverted by the arrival of none other than Duffy's Circus to the town.

With the whole place exploding in a riot of sound and colour. I mean, why would anyone be bothered with the likes of that silly old Edgar Wallace, with his black-and-white and grey dismal tales of people in trench coats shuffling around foggy London – when, right on your doorstep, what did you have – only a veritable feast of non-stop entertainment?

& all in living full colour as a Mexican-style anaconda of humans made its way down the main street accompanied by a fanfare of trumpets, with no end of painted wagons, fire-eaters, balloons and candy-striped awnings.

Not to mention the *pièce de resistance, le big top magnifico* being erected with great ceremony in the Fair Green Field – where a procession of multicoloured carnival heads, familiar faces from stage and screen, led Duffy's Circus Hollywood Jamboree through the open gate, with a great grey elephant standing proudly on guard.

And with poster after poster decorating every available inch of space along the main street, promising snow-white ponies 'all the way from Arabia' – and a lion by the name of Goldie who could devour a grown man's head in seconds.

Also on the bill were a considerable complement of clowns – jugglers and Maria Santini the trapeze artist from Bologna.

Yes, it certainly was a riot of fun and games in our town at that time – with John Steed out of *The Avengers*, in his carnival head, drinking pints along with Patrick McGoohan from *The Prisoner*, sitting up at the counter in The Tower Select Bar.

So, as you can imagine, I was nowhere to be seen in the vicinity of our house, never mind being busy standing sentry over wardrobes – no matter how much I might love our famous coins.

One of the great things as regards The Famous Hollywood Jamboree was that you could lie in that Fair Green Field all day on your back – and, free, gratis and for nothing, amuse yourself by listening to the limitless parade of tunes that came pouring thick and fast from the flaring bells of the mounted shiny speakers – including one by a group called The Seekers, soaring high above that daisy-studded meadow and off out among the dripping trees. Yes, *the carnival is over*, they kept on insisting.

Except that what you had to say about that particular smug bout of vehemence was that, in fact, all it amounted to was one hilarious, absolutely side-splitting joke! With the truth, of course, being that the festivities – why, they had not even yet properly commenced!

With – as if the intention was to prove that very point – who comes poking his nose around a freighter than only the one and only tousle-haired comedian Charlie Drake:

–'Ello, my darlings! Any of you 'appen to 'ave seen my boomerang? Because I'm sorry to say, for some 'stwange weason', it 'ain't come back!

Before running off through the sideshows, slugging from a bottle of Guinness.

As a squadron of insects attacked me on the face and neck – and The Seekers continued, with an obstinacy truly absurd, to insist on the imminent conclusion of all festivities – in spite of the fact that everyone knew it was set to continue for a further three days!

–Now then, lads and lassies! Come along, close it down now, Seekers! Ee-urgh! Ee-urgh!

As a certain contemporary of theirs might have observed. And who at that time, of course, was riding high in the charts – no, not much talk of disabled wards then!

During that time when the whole world was rosy and the carnival proper hadn't even actually begun – never mind come to an end, you idiot lot, Seekers! As perhaps you might have understood had you happened to be in the vicinity of the Tower Bar public house that very evening when the double doors swung open and in trooped Sausage the world-famous clown, followed by a train of kazoo-parping enthusiasts, not least among whom was the popular TV singing star Val Doonican, performing a funny swaying walk as he sat on the bar in his carnival head – just like you'd see him on the telly, in his V-neck diamond-patterned sweater and casual fawn slacks.

–You are all very welcome to come along tonight to enjoy both myself and my colleagues performing here at The Duffy's Circus Follies, in what is to be the triumph of our touring season. Because, make no mistake, we have a host of stars

assembled for you here in this little town of yours tonight.
Including …!

Morecambe and Wise
Double Trouble
The Kaye Sisters
Three in Harmony
Jimmy Clitheroe
The Clitheroe Kid
Ted Lune
Lancashire's Long Laugh
Peter Sinclair
Cock O' the North
Margo Henderson
Impressions at the Piano
The Demijeans
Two Boys and a Girl

−Yes! he squealed, uproariously clapping his hands.

After which, the Saturday night singing star hopped once
more down off the stool and was in the process of leading his
gay troupe off again on their travels − when the door was flung
open, and in rushed Coco in a red triangular hat, holding a
basin of water − putting on this great big deep exaggerated bass
voice, as he suspended the vessel momentarily above his head:

Oh, do you know the muffin man
The muffin man, the muffin man
Do you know the muffin man
Who lives in Drury Lane?

−Here, I say! demanded Sausage − just where do you think
you're going with that basin of water?

As *splash!* down it went over poor Val Doonican's head.

And off they went into the street, performing the conga.

150

So, hardly any wonder then that the younger Frank B. would ecstatically peal:

–Hooray for the hooplas and all the gaily coloured swing-boats, yes please can we hear it once more for the swirling calliope and the hobbies with their fierce shining enamel smiles – as out we shout *whee!* and the thoughts in our heads become as stars in that sky of warm blue stretched high, away over the town.

–So the carnival is over, then, is it? I said, as I chucked the pink ball and managed to strike Mr Coconut a good hard blow – as down he plummets, like a woebegone Gonk.

–Because that is where you are wrong, my old friends The Seekers! Wronger than you'll ever know!

Before looking around to see a long-standing friend of my father's, locally known as 'The Weasel' Finnegan.

Who had, quite literally, appeared out of nowhere, nego-tiating his passage through the narrowest of gaps between a flatbed trailer and the heavy canvas slapping against the tent's braced supports.

His face was covered completely in oil.

–C'mere you! I heard him shout, as he crooked his finger, get over here till I talk to you!

He fired up a Woodbine cigarette and swore that, as long as he lived, he'd never take the job of an Indian again.

–No! This is the end of the line for Finnegan! he vowed.

Then, sweeping defiantly out of his hip pocket, came a naggin of whiskey, which he shook threateningly at a white-plumed pony.

–Does auld Duffy think that The Weasel comes cheap? Can he really be serious when he asks me to run around wearing this fuck of a thing?

He tore off the red-and-white big chief war bonnet and tramped it remorselessly into the dirt.

—Well, that's it then – I'm off for sure. And if you do happen
to see auld Mr Duffy or any of the rest of that no-good clan of
his – just you tell them that The Weasel won't be back today or
any other day – *comprende, kemo sabe?*

Then he wandered off through the squelchy muck, tumbling
over a guy rope just before he made it to the exit.

As I smiled to myself and followed him, heading homeward.

Looking forward to telling that old Da about all the adventures I'd enjoyed at the circus – principally those involving
his friend, the notoriously unreliable council labourer stroke
Indian Brave.

Yes, we were going to have a great old laugh, I thought.

That is, I considered, whenever I eventually did manage to
make it home.

Because, in those days in the town, you really used to meet
so many people.

Everyone with something to say.

About the town and all their lives.

The things that happened and all those that might.

—There you are, Frank!

—Yes, indeed, here I am.

—A grand old circus, am I to understand?

—Yes, without question, a grand old topping entertainment
extravaganza!

—You have to hand it to Mr Duffy!

—Yes, you absolutely do indeed!

—Well, good luck now, Frank!

—G'luck now, colleagues – all the best!

& then, of course, your own pals – namely Joe and Philip and,
of course, Saucy Bunn – which wasn't her real name, of course, but
who was going to know that seeing as she came from England.

& said that she'd auditioned for a part on the telly. Putting on this Dusty Springfield voice and doing a dance in and out between the puddles.

—*Oi'll give it foive*! she shouted as she leapt on top of Conaty's wall, holding up two imaginary cards.

One for a hit and another for a miss.

She wore a dress with all squares on it and every time you seen her, her eyes were done up different – this time looking all sooty with mascara.

—I live in Landin! she said, it's not like here. Did you ever hear of the Two I's Club?

Knowing full well that none of us had, which was why she asked the question.

Then she was gone, snapping her fingers and *la-la-la-ing* all the way down the lane, only this time sounding like Sandie Shaw.

With the last thing I remember about the end of that particularly wonderful day at the circus being the purchase and most eager consumption of a certain item of refreshment on the premises of a certain Mary Conaty – namely one Palm Grove ice pop, or 'lolly' – complete with its neat little football shirt of thin 'n' tasty chocolate.

—You like the Palm Grove, I remember Mary remarking on that occasion, with her eyes crinkling up at the corners the way they used to.

—I do indeed, I had gamely replied, and that's for sure! I think perhaps that it may well be my favourite!

—Ah, that's nice to hear, our Frank, she said, in a manner soft and quiet not dissimilar to Grace Courtney.

They were rare fun times – none better, thanks to the carnival.

& the committed labours of the tireless Mr Duffy.

As I sighed and pushed the front door open.

& then got a thump in face, which briefly stunned me.

Not surprisingly, since it had arrived completely out of nowhere.

Because you usually don't expect your old Da to be waiting there for you – in the hall, I mean, and not looking one bit like the old father that you usually saw, but like someone who had come in and taken over possession.

Then what happens, doesn't the statue of the Infant of Prague standing above on the fanlight, come flying down and hit me on the side of the head.

It was lying there looking at me as Da gave me a push and then another bash.

–Tell me where you've hidden the fucking coins! he says, with his eyes blazing as he rubbed his knuckles – then it will be easier for us all.

He moaned a few more times after that.

Before my mother came in and just stood there – remained there, staring, toying with the brush & saying nothing.

–Just answer the question when I ask you, will you, he said – very softly this time – just tell me, please, where it is that you've put them? Go on.

I made no reply. My head was spinning.

With the facts of the matter being that I didn't know.

–I'll give you till the count of three, he said, as he turned around and looked at her, leaning on top of the brush, making a crutch.

–Maybe you have some idea, do you? As mother, wide-eyed, shook her head, walking her fingers up and down the length of the wooden broom-handle.

Then he turned back to me and I heard him roar:

–The coins! I said, did you not hear me? The coins, I said!

As he closed his fist and drew back his arm.

–Whumph!

So that was the day at the circus, with it transpiring in the end that he'd gone and hidden them away himself, and then completely forgotten.

He must have stayed up all the rest of the night – I could hear him moving around downstairs in the kitchen, muttering and arguing with himself – but in a voice so far from his funny W.C. Fields one that it might have been an entirely different person.

–Duffy's Circus, he kept on repeating, don't talk to me about fucking Duffy's Circus!

Then all went silent – and I concluded that he must have fallen asleep, like he sometimes did, with one shoe hanging off, on the sofa.

With the joke, of course, of the whole thing being that, a couple of weeks after the carnival had moved on, who did I meet when I was going up the town – 'The Weasel' Finnegan, alias Navajo Joe.

–Ah, good man Frank! he says as soon as he seen me, you'll never believe this but who am I after talking to this minute? Only your very own father, aye your own auld Da Brady – and fresh and well he's looking, I have to say.

As he dropped a handful of coins into a puddle and said that my father had given them to him.

–They're going to be worth a lot of money some day, he said, and he ought to know, for he's an expert. Isn't that right, son?

Then he was gone, through the doors of the Tower Bar, explaining how my father had given him the bag of coins for safe-keeping – and then gone and forgotten all about it.

& that night, I dreamed about The Weasel Finnegan, consuming huge purple hoops of fire, one after the other – before producing, with a flamboyant flourish, a single solitary newly-minted coin from his pocket and holding it up between his finger and his thumb.

Inspecting it carefully as he rotated it in front of a mesmerised audience, as a drumroll sounded and he took a bow.

–That, ladies and gentlemen, is what you call numismatology!

As I heard my name being called and looked up to see The Weasel with his two eyes bulging and one of the trapezes wound around his neck, swaying to and fro as the saxophone continued.

& I can't really say whether or not it was a premonition – but I got some more results from my tests the next day, confirming that yes, I was now, without a doubt, Stage 4.

Not that it bothered me, at least not initially – with me even doing drawings that I've included in the final magazine.

I don't know if you remember the Gonks – stars of Beatland in the film they made – & now, somewhat unexpectedly, to the fore in much of my cancer artwork.

& I have to say that they do look good – sort of like tiny little coconuts with wriggly spider legs, only now dressed in chemical suits like you'd see in *E. T.*, hosing down walls in case of contamination.

With all these spores now running wild right through your body – at least that was what I thought – although Mrs Beacon said I was exaggerating.

–You're only getting yourself into a state, she said, my love.

& which I liked to hear, because it had been a long time since anyone had said the like of that.

My love, I mean.

But the more I tried to get rid of them, the more Gonks there seemed to be.

Until every fucking one of them in the world seemed to have arrived – gliding along in these midget submarines, surging forward in silver flotillas.

With one of them, in particular, pressing his face up against the window, covered in blood – with it all smeared across his face as he lifted up an ice pick – grinning hideously as he pointed it directly at me.

–You're for the chop, Mr Brady, I'm afraid, I heard him say.

At the exact same time as a junior doctor went bustling past – and, before I knew it, I'd caught a hold of him by the arm and was roaring at him, acting the very same as Da.

–Why didn't medical science do something for my mother – eaten by rats at the bottom of a fucking lake? Why couldn't they have done something about that, Doc?

In the end, however, Mrs Beacon managed to calm me down.

With the pair of us enjoying a great laugh about the Gonks.

But I can't imagine what might have happened – if Mrs Beacon hadn't been there, I mean.

Because the junior doctor – he had definitely been badly shaken.

But whatever Mary said to the consultant, in the end they agreed not to notify the hospital.

What a wonderful woman she was – because anyone else would probably have decided to have nothing more to do with me.

Instead of buying me sandwiches at the kiosk and sitting there distracting me, suggesting that maybe we could go on holiday.

–Maybe one day, she said, in another time. In another world.

& that was the reason I found myself on Paradise Island, leading a baby monkey along on a halter, as we made our way slowly across the white sand to where my father and mother were waiting, underneath a lush green, swaying tree.

Terminal is a horrible word.

But not with Mrs Beacon it wasn't.

I think, in a way, maybe I loved her.

That day, anyway, I did for sure.

& why I was able for six hours' work on the trot – scribbling out Stage 4, which I must have written at least five hundred times, and replacing it with something infinitely more light-hearted — a matchstick picture of the one and only:

Slave Robot from Mars

Accompanied by this little made-up story, which really did put a smile on my face, I have to say. I hope you like it.

The very minute that Fudsy Budlett, aged nine, of The Terrace, The Universe, Earth, The World, walked into his workshop, Grandpa Buddlers knew immediately that something was up.

When Fudsy called on him, the boy was usually full of beans, and skipped his way down the path to the workshop, shouting that he was there.

This time he wandered in, stole up to the workbench and murmured: 'Hello, Grandpa.'

Fudsy's father's father was seventy-five. He was a very spry old man and, in his retirement, he had two interests; his family, of which Fudsy was an important member, and his hobby of making and cobbling together robots. He had been a robot technician all his life.

'Well, Fudsy boy, how is everything?'

Fudsy stared out of the window and watched the fly cars dropping down to the landing platforms at the edge of the city. Grandpa's place was almost in the open country.

'Oh,' said Fudsy. 'Alright.'

'That means it's not,' said the old man. 'How are Father and Mother?'

'Oh. fine. Mother got her new house robot today.'

'Ah, that's good. Now she'll be able to take things easier. So she should, after all that time in hospital.'

'Yes,' said Fudsy, 'but …' he hesitated, '… that means that I shan't be able to have my own robot, like all of the other boys. Dad said it would be years before he paid off the money on the house robot.'

Grandpa knew that Fudsy loved his parents, even though he hadn't properly looked after his father when he died, & not been there when his mother fell into the water with the rats, but he understood that it hurt to be one of the few boys who did not come to school with a personal robot to carry books and to give him a rub down after games and gym and to run other little errands.

'What about that pal of yours — Joe Purcell, wasn't it? Who didn't have a robot either?'

'That's right.'

Fudsy wandered into the little workroom. On the bench was the carcass of a big robot, its head and front off, with the wiring of the chest section exposed.

Grandpa followed.

'Now, there's a puzzle. I bought him in a job lot of junk recently, and I've only just got around to taking a look at him.'

'Why's he a puzzle?'

'Because I've never seen anything like him. You know that that all robots under the laws of 2350 have to have the maker's name and their aptitude grade marked? Well, this one's got no markings at all.'

'That means,' said Fudsy, 'that he's over five hundred years old!'

'Yes. First time I've ever had anything to do with such an ancient piece.'

Fudsy stared at the machine. It was certainly bigger and clumsier-looking than present models.

'What's the difference between this one and the ones of today?'

'Far as I can gather,' said his grandfather, 'these early robots were just like imitation men, whereas the models available to us now, in the present day, Fudsy, no matter how closely you inspect them, there is very little difference between them and the average, real-life human person.'

'Then they might as well be functioning, living human beings,' deduced Fudsy. 'Strange.'

'Yes, very strange indeed,' repeated his grandfather.

I closed the computer, feeling extremely satisfied indeed now that my adventures in space were concluded.

Or so it seemed.

***

Certainly as I lay there on my bed later on – not paying so much as a whit of attention to the stars and the planets that roamed far overhead, high above the town and The Terrace – not even, in fact, giving a hoot whether space or the stars had even ever existed, just wanting everything around me in the lane to be alright.

And which I knew, somehow, it would be – because that was the sort of humour I was in – and which was why I was more than grateful to the slave robot and all of his crazy old antics.

As I sighed and cradled my hands behind my head – and then saw my old pals coming along with their bags of marbles.

That was when my heart started to pound – sensing that I knew what was coming.

The dread, that is.

With the shadow of the priest, Fr Dominic, falling ever so slowly.

& the squeak of his shoes as he made his way towards them – all along the length of the lane.

With his fist tightly closed in behind his flapping soutane.

Just standing there, staring, as the boys crouched down – and the taw went scudding in a flickering trail of light.

–I've got something for you, I heard Fr Dominic say – and that was when I covered my eyes.

And that familiar old sweat, with all its prickles, began trailing down the side of my face.

–Oh no, I said.

As the priest moved forward.

–I think you'll find I've got something for you, I heard him say again – only this time, softer.

Then he reached out and opened his hand.

I was all choked up.

–Look, said Joe suddenly, it's a snowdrop, and it's growing.

Right in the centre of the priest's hand as he stood there.

–I've never seen anything like it, Joe said.

& then, when we looked, Fr Dominic was gone.

When you make things up, it can sometimes be wonderful – even if it's only silly robots from Mars.

& that's why I couldn't wait to get at it again – because you never know what's going to come out.

Things as beautiful as Fr Dominic and his flower, which reminded me, with its little white bell head nodding in the breeze, of Da handing you a penny in the doorway of some pub, and telling you how happy they had been one time, him and Ma.

Or 'your mother', as he called her in such situations.

& that's what you're always hoping for, I suppose – a little tale like that to take wing and make you happy.

With the only problem being that you can never be sure.

As I discovered the following morning, having expected to type up 'Robot Slave Part 2'.

Sitting down at my desk as I rolled up my sleeves and shouted out:

–Go to it, J.J.!

Before realising – as I've since, more or less, come to accept – that, when it came to typing out stories, I didn't seem to be in charge of fucking anything.

Without sight nor sign of any slave robot to be seen.

Sometimes it can frighten you, the unexpected way it can happen.

Master Googleboy's Magnificent Adventures
(Fun with Science: Visions of the Future)

It was a fine old day in the middle of the summer and now that it was the future, Fudsy Budlett of The Terrace had never felt so good in his life.

Because what you had in the future was jetpacks, fly cars and telephones with Skype that you can click on to surf on Google and the web and talk to anyone you like – at any minute of night or day.

That's you in the future — because you are the boss.

Of all the different things you can have — whether Google Glass, Google Earth, or any of these other devices that enable you to see visions — the likes of which, in the past you'd never have dreamed.

& which is why Googleboy is laughing, because now that he is going back to the past, he is away off out to his garage to gather up some knick-knacks to assist him on his journey.

& which include some old-style wing mirrors, the likes of which you might see on a Morris Minor, and a pair of great big milk-bottle glasses, something like maybe Troy Tempest might wear.

As away he went with all his things in a bag, back through the wastes of time and space and coming flying in to land over the roofs of the town where he was born and where it all, long ago, used to happen.

They were sure all going to get a laugh when he knocked on the door and they found him standing there on the step with these big glasses and bike helmet and would probably not believe him with all his news about the future. Saying Googleboy, vamoose, get out of here with all that malarkey, for what you look like is something you might see in Duffy's Circus — maybe getting shot from a cannon or something, but definitely not a messenger from the future.

163

'Yes, this is just the greatest laugh ever,' they would say.

Falling around on the step as they chortled.

But they soon wouldn't say that when Googleboy got into his stride — with all the knowledge he had about inventions — whether that meant Wi-Fi, webcams, VR headsets or anything else — he soon would have them interested in his 'informations'.

Yes, for once, Fudsy Budlett would be the boss & king of all.

& that was sure going to be something to look forward to.

As in he glided on his jetpack Google machine & wasted no time in going around to Joe Purcell's house.

Who, understandably, was taken aback to see him — because it isn't every day a fellow from the future drops by.

'Googleboy! I can't believe it was you all along, Francie, so I can't,' he said. 'I have to say you really had me fooled. But it's sure good to see you.'

Then he said, 'Let's go around to Philip.'

'Yes, that's a good idea,' I said. As around to the square we went to our old friend.

'Boy, I can't believe it,' said Joe, 'you turning up like that, from tomorrow.'

'Life is sure full of surprises,' I said.

& he said it sure was.

Then we went knock knock on the door.

As we looked in the window to see that Philip's mother — she was baking cakes!

'Mm! They look tasty!' said Joe.

'Well, boy, if that isn't a good one,' Googleboy said as he and his oldest friend laughed and laughed.

Because you have to remember — they were blood-brother Injuns.

As in they went and then in came Philip. Having just that minute finished his homework, he said.

'Blessed sums,' he said, 'ha ha.'

'Ha ha,' we laughed, 'those blessed old sums.'

It was great to hear Philip talking just like of old, thought Googleboy. 'It sure is good to see you, Philip — to see you again after all this time. How are you?'

'I'm good,' said Philip, 'excellent really, Googleboy.'

'Excellent, are you?' said Googleboy, 'that's terrific.'

With them all then asking him to tell them about the future, because they'd never met before anyone from there.

'Not me anyway,' Joe said, morosely.

But with Googleboy saying he was afraid that if he started, he might not be able to know when to finish.

'Still, that's OK,' said Philip. 'Isn't it, Joe?'

& Joe said yes — that that was fine.

'It's OK, Googleboy,' said Philip, 'Go ahead.'

As off went the visitor — with him being in the middle of all these stories about there never ever going to be banknotes again and drones that could deliver your messages right to your house — when the door opened softly and who pops his head in only that good old Mr Nugent, the head of the home, with his pipe peeping out of his breast pocket.

Before he took it out and began packing baccy into its bowl, as he shook his head and said to him: 'Googleboy, you're not going to tell me that they're doing away with tobacco. Because I couldn't just imagine a world without Maltan Ready Rubbed.'

Everyone laughed when they heard him saying that.

'But it would disappear,' their visitor insisted, 'and it's not the only thing, either, I can tell you.'

As they shook their heads, amazed, bewildered by all that Googleboy had to tell them.

'Cash coming out of a hole in the wall?' said Mr Nugent, 'I just can't believe what I'm hearing, Master Googleboy!'

'Yes,' affirmed Googleboy, 'and robots performing operations like surgeons.'

'It's a shocking state of affairs,' said Mr Nugent resignedly, 'all these things that the future is getting up to.'

'But that's not all, because there's good things too.' Googleboy added. 'With the best of them all being that we can correct the past.'

'Correct the past?' said Mr Nugent.

'Yes,' nodded Googleboy, 'to make whatever wrongs you might have done come right.'

'Well, that is quite a discovery, I have to say, Googleboy. But surely doing that — such as, for example, reversing what you did to my poor wife — to make that possible …' He stared sadly down at the floor. 'Surely, Googleboy, that cannot be?'

'But it can,' said Googleboy, as he reached in his pocket and pulled out a bleeper-booly. & which, he said, all you had to do with was bleep bleep booly and another bleep bleep and then Mrs Nugent there, she would be alive again.

Just hanging out washing, the very exact same as before.

Or baking cakes, which she actually, now, wasn't doing.

Because, of course, the truth was she was still dead: with PIGS all written over the walls, in her family's memories. And which they had never stopped thinking about, since.

But now all that was about to change.

With bleep bleep booly and another bleep bleep — and her head appearing, magically, back on her shoulders.

Which would see visitor Googleboy becoming once more the hero of the hour — only this time, for good — having been the man who had bleeped Mrs Nugent back into living colour again, with everyone cheering him up there in the dock.

Shouting: 'Set him free!'

& Googleboy: 'Hooray!'

Except that when he removed his Googly Earth glasses, which he'd been using in the course of his explanations, Googleboy was shaken by the realisation of what he was seeing.

Because the Nugent family — they were gone, and in their place, along with Joe, there were three great pigs, fat as fools, still sitting in the armchairs but glaring at him fiercely, in silence, with tiny black studs in place of eyes.

Ones that were entirely bereft of pity.

As Mr Nugent — in a voice like a Dalek — emptied out his pipe and said: 'We want to hear no more of these schemes, or any of this nonsense about the future you've been telling us. We know well who you are and of what it is you are more than capable. Because we are the Nugents and we know the bitter truth — that, for us, there isn't any future and the past is always the present. For the simple reason that you made it that way. So, go to hell, whoever you are, so-called Master Googleboy — back to those days of the future, or wherever it is that you belong. For it certainly isn't here. Isn't that right, Joseph?'

```
    As  Joe  Purcell  nodded  and  came  over  to
shake hands with Googleboy.
    Except, instead of doing that, he ripped
off a wing mirror and flung it, coldly, into
the fire.
    So that was the end of — bleep bleep! —
Googleboy's  fabulous  adventures,  for  the
moment.
```

∗∗∗

I don't really like playing Snakes & Ladders all that much on my own, especially in the night when you can hear Toddy Ray – Mrs Beacon's pride and joy, with it turning out that he's dying, like myself.

And it's not just that there can't be a winner, but because there isn't anyone there to distract you from staring at the squares, which I have always liked to do, right from when I was very young – altogether a hundred pictures.

For example, if Ricky Shabs was here, he would no sooner have started shaking and rattling the dice in the cup before he'd say:

–Bro'! Do you think maybe Keith Duffy would like to be in my movie?

This is because he's seen him in *Robocroc*, and is reminded by the fish that he sees in square no. 21 – where shoals of them are going floating past underneath the waves.

Or it could be the little red rocket with its orange booster jets firing as it heads away off on a mission into outer space, with the twinkling stars frozen far away there in the blue being more than enough to set him off on an entirely different train of thought – involving some programme he has seen on TV about aliens and pyramids or just what might be really going on in the Nevada desert in Area 51. As he temporarily abandons our tournament and begins to pace the floor of the office, with his big head jerking and his fingers snapping away as he gathers his thoughts – with it all being 'bro' this and 'bro' the other, before he finally gets fed up and sits back down.

But which, at least, as I say, always manages to take my mind off something new, which I'd have seen in one of the squares – like this pool of stunning colour into which I allow myself to dive, & which you'd be afraid you might never come out of.

What exactly it could be that I'd see, I don't really know, because it's different every time – not surprisingly, considering the many attractive options, including Hickory Dickory, Humpty Dumpty, the Three Blind Mice and so on.

But I suppose it could be some small unnoticed detail of the cupboard Mrs Hubbard goes in and finds empty, and which you can see on square no. 23 – or the pie out of which all the black-birds come flying.

With you sometimes being so hypnotised by it that it can almost erase your whole being and body as you sit there – and away you go right inside that little frame – just the very same as I used to when I was small.

Only, just as often, becoming so wandering and wayward in your mind that, before you even realise what it is you're doing, you have advanced your counter three or four squares and – lo and behold – you're away down a snake.

And which always seems to happen when you have allowed your mind to become unmoored like that – although there never seemed to be very many ladders parked on the squares that you used to arrive at – & up which you could shoot in order to win a prize.

Certainly not that I can remember.

And that's the sort of way it is now – or at least it was a couple of squares ago – when I moved the pink counter to land on Bunny Cuddles.

Or what me and Ma used to always call me – Bunny Cuddles, at that time on Saturday evenings when we played. Which is not to say that we did so regularly. In fact, altogether maybe only two or three times because, you have to remember, after all, that my Ma, God rest her soul, she had enough on her plate in those days without running up ladders and sliding down snakes.

But anyhow, there we were – sitting at the table in the kitchen by the window, with Ma clapping her hands as the fire flickered softly in the grate, before she let out this unmerciful squeal:

–Bunny Cuddles, do you see what it is that you have just done? Why, you've only gone and landed on the square with the jam!

And by which she meant, my own private and personal panel – where our favourite lop-eared grey rabbit was sitting on the tiles spooning dollops of it into him – yes, great big spoonfuls of strawberry out of a pot.

& boy did he seem to be enjoying it!

That was where she had got her name for me – and now, here we were, having landed on that very same picture again.

But with that just being the start of it – because when I closed my left eye and squinted – what did I see only the bottom rung of a ladder.

As – *whoosh*! – away I went, like billy-o, up to the very top rung and arriving proudly at frame no. 11 – where Simple Simon was already halfway down the road, making his way to the fair.

While my eyes misted over – and yes, as I say, why here it was coming again, as I knew well it would – that very same lovely delicious feeling, which somehow managed, without you even trying, to make the world that you lived in – and everything around you at that particular moment in time – become as bright and DeLuxe-coloured as the small paintings right there on the board in front of you.

And which was why, without even having to try, I could see myself coming strolling down the street – every bit as happy as Larry, whoever he was supposed to be.

Yes, passing those same old sights – the petrol pumps with their Esso sign and the old broken fountain that had been built in honour of the Queen – except that she hadn't even bothered her arse putting in an appearance.

Not that I cared a jot whether she had or whether she hadn't, being far too busy calling out to Mary in her shop – or, outside it, rather, lifting a bale of *Evening Herald*s at the door.

–That's not a bad day, I called, as she looked over.

–It is not indeed, she replied, I think it's going to keep dry for Sunday.

Whatever was on on Sunday, I thought – probably some big match or other, at which she would sell a big pile of papers.

Then who goes by only Mickey the Night.

–That's not a bad night, he says, although I'd say that it's got cauld!

That's what he always said – whether it happened to be day or night.

As Jaunty McCoy rattled past with his bike.

–Pack of mean, no-good, rotten lousy cunts! he says, without even bothering to look in my direction.

Whoever they were.

Then who's arrived, unfolding her umbrella – only Mrs Packie Carroll, shaking out some drops that had been trapped inside.

–You can never be too careful, Bunny Cuddles! she calls across, so if I were you, my fine young chap, I'd pop back to The Terrace and retrieve my own umbrella.

–Right you be, Mrs Packie! I said.

As she gave me a smile and said:

–It's nice to see you home, Bunny Cuddles. Were you away?

—I was indeed, Mrs Packie, I said, away there for a while.

—But now you're back!

—Back is right – back, for sure – here I am!

—That's good, she says, and away off then in her rain hood, grinding her gums.

So all that was good.

But nothing to what I discovered was coming next – as I stood there and knocked on the front door of the Purcells – where Joe and his mother and sisters lived, now that his father had, sadly, passed away.

Joe had been my oldest friend once – before I committed the mistake that ruined me.

But there wasn't gonna be any talk about that now.

As rap rap rap I went on the door – and to my astonishment being admitted to find all the Nugents sitting around the table – even Mrs Nugent, the woman whose life I'd taken.

So that, I have to say, was surely a surprise.

Not that they seemed to think so – even, can you believe it, the poor unfortunate murdered victim.

—It's nice to see you, said Mrs Nugent, in her scarf and hat.

—Thank you, I said.

As Mrs Purcell said:

—I'll take your coat, Francie.

There was even a robin at the window, staring.

And it did my heart good when I heard him thrillingly erupt:

—Three jolly hoorays for the arrival of Bunny Cuddles!

—I've just put a fresh pot on this very minute, said Mrs Nugent.

Meaning tea, of course.

As we all sat then in a circle, chatting away about the world in general.

Before Mrs Joe Purcell came back in and suddenly said:

—Here now! Would anyone fancy a little piece of pie?

As she twinkled a little and looked right across at me.

—I think, over there, is a certain little rabbit who wouldn't say no to an offer the like of that! Would I be correct there, Bunny, what do you say?

And I really had to laugh.

Ah yes, it was a good old time, as those dreams always are.

Before you flick, yes, you give your eyelids a little flick and — *hey presto!* — what has happened only all of them are gone.

And not just the Purcells and the Nugents either — but the fountain for the Queen, the Esso sign and the petrol pumps and everything.

Yes, you can say goodbye to your colour by DeLuxe — as the remainder of the bright blues and reds and olive greens ebb away, and the pink plastic button of the counter underneath your thumb remains steadfastly obstinate on the tessellated cardboard sheet.

And continues to remain that way — with all your efforts coming to nothing.

Before, without even so much as a hint of warning, it suddenly shoots forward — and you find yourself devoured by the dripping, slavering mouth of a python — then travelling, for centuries, it seems, through a world of lunar strangeness, where corpuscles bearing the faces of your loved ones observe you with disinterest, coming together to form what seems like a great big patch of seaweed — before opening their mouths to speak, except that you are destined never to hear what it is they might be saying, having already been devoured by a passing giant jellyfish — and then regurgitated into the dead centre of the no. 1 square — with one single word, in vivid blush pink, hovering waveringly, directly over your head:

PIG

Chapter 17

A Song of Praise

It really can take you a while to get used to the word 'terminal'.

Or even to become just a little bit comfortable with it.

Constantly thinking – at least in the beginning – now is the time, I've definitely had it today.

& then as soon as you got so much as hint of a twinge or an ache in your stomach, you'd be away off thinking, I see they're back on the move again – meaning them dastardly old Gonky cancer-distributing aquamen – piloting downstream in their flippers and visors, making very little sound at all apart from an uprising gurgling tail of bubbles.

& the interior of your body becoming more and more like outer space the more you thought about it, and just as eerie – your lungs and other parts ominously studded with little patches of carbon as onward plunged the school of relentless miniature sea-commandos.

–Gonks on patrol! I said to Mrs Beacon.

However, she just smiled faintly, making out she hadn't heard a word I'd said.

But I could make light of it all I liked, because sometimes when they piloted in close, you could see their eyes, black as pearls, in behind the blurred glass of their visors – & sometimes they might remind me of Tommy the Weaver.

–Why did you take my knife? they said, do you think that's good, stealing from a dying man?

& I know that during that period, I was becoming very short with people – even with Mrs Beacon, sometimes.

& definitely with Ricky Shabs.

Who threatened not to have anything more to do with me.

–Fuck you, bro'! I remember him saying, you has got the attitude!

But, fortunately, we patched it up – and he was in again this morning, asking me to look something up.

Because, as far as he is concerned, he says, the whole World Trade Centre tragedy was a set-up, and Bin Laden and Bush had been working together all along.

Yes, in recent times you don't hear a word about any of that, or anything else about the Twin Towers – unless you happen to run into a certain conspiracy theorist, who happens to go by the name of His Majesty Ricky Shabs.

It was the American military who had blown up the Towers, he says, with the buildings coming down as a result of a controlled explosion.

And maybe he's right – I couldn't really say.

Because I don't have all that much politics in the magazine.

But, having realised just how wrong I had been in the hospital – until Mrs Beacon made me see sense – I have to say:

–I'm sorry, Shabs, but I just don't buy it.

Because even a government led by the greatest fucking Gonk of them all, Donald Trump – are they really going to be dumb enough to go and take a risk like that, murder their own citizens?

Sorry, Rick The Shabs, but I'm afraid it ain't gonna fly.

He has somehow managed to link it up with aliens – and some crash-landing spacecraft they discovered in Nevada – in Area 51.

I don't know, I was saying.

I really couldn't say for sure, Ricky Shabs.

& then he starts laughing and falling on top of the bed.

–Oh man, that is so wicked! he says, and points at the picture I've been working on, on the screen.

& which I wasn't going to include but I think, for sure, I definitely will now.

–Old school, you has gots to put him on YouTube, bro'!

& which I might have done, sure – if I wasn't so pressed for time – because come tomorrow, I am so going to be history around here!

Octopi – Interesting Facts

Somewhere in California — a scientist is busy scratching his head.

Wondering what the devil is going on in the aquarium.

As he and his colleagues mount a nightly vigil — &, to their astonishment, discover an amazing fact!

Finding themselves staring in mute disbelief at the spectacle of a very small octopus, or cephalopod, not so much as making a sound as he adroitly pushes the lid of a glass tank open, and soundlessly slides out onto the floor before making his way across the room towards another tank filled with the rarest specimens of tropical fish.

Before winding his tentacle in among the beautiful creatures and — *thlupp* — up comes a helpless, rainbow-coloured guppy as Olly shoves it right down the hatch.

More amazing facts coming next week, readers!

Except, you see, that there won't – because I won't be sitting here at my desk or anywhere else – for the simple reason that I'll be en route to Paradise Island, having printed my very first inaugural hot-off-the-presses copy of *The Big Yaroo* for all of you to read,

& hopefully enjoy.

But, before I do that, I want to give you the rest of the details of my story, & what went on that fatal night long ago in Dublin – the true facts about Gardiner St., that is.

Not the ridiculous version that was peddled at the time by Scotty Haggis Windsor Davis & Co.

Welcome to *The Case of the Lonely Widow*, another made-up pile of bullshit by Edgar Wallace Pictures – starring Windsor Haggis as The Dumb Detective.

& Clocker Kiernan as himself.

–You can tell me, the clinical director says, after all that's what I'm here for Frank, is it not? twisting a button this way & then the other.

–Yes, I know, Clinical Director, I responded.

But didn't say anything more after that.

As the big Frank investigation continues and now what's happening – a female officer!

& which I have to say was nice, as I nibbled away at the bun they'd just given me.

Nice tasty icing along the top and around the edges.

–*Sweet magnifico*! I said as she knelt beside me.

–So what's the story, Juliet Bravo? I said.

Well, I'm sorry to disappoint you, but I'm afraid that I did not.

& instead just carried on munching away at my cake.

–You're enjoying that, she says, and I nodded.

Then she asked me a couple more questions.

About Grace and the break-in and how long exactly I'd been watching the shop.

–Look, I said, officer, there was only one reason I went in there that night – because of the Twin Towers, the city was crawling with police! I mean – what else could I have done?

–I see, she replied, but you could tell that she didn't believe me.

–But it's funny now, isn't it – thinking about all those Russians! I laughed.

–Russians, she said.

–Russians who weren't Russians – who turned out to be Romanians!

–Romanians, she said.

–Here come the Russians – except that they're not Russians at all!

–Not Russians.

–The Russians, I chuckled, yes the Russians, the Russians, the Russians are not coming at all!

–Shut your fucking mouth! says Davies.

& looks like he's about to have a stroke.

Or '*aboot to hae*' one, as I said to him, looking over.

As he glared at me again and, like before, insisted he wasn't Scottish.

But I knew that anyway, all along.

Frae Tipperary or summat, hee hee hee.

By now all the icing on the bun had gone.

–Any chance of another? I said to PC Bravo.

She shook her head.

–You have got to be fucking joking, says Windsor, plum-red.

As Bravo just stands there, with her hands placed on her hips.

She was now a bit pale-looking too.

–Where did you get the knife from? she inquires.

I felt like saying: is that not your job? But then I thought: you know what, it isn't worth it.

Because detectives these days, they're just gone to the dogs.

& not a bit like that old Fabian in his heyday.

Or any of those other Edgar Wallace-style old-timers.

With their stupid body-warmers, Puffa jackets and fucking headsets. The modern guys.

Give you the pip.

–Why did you hit him? she says.

& I'd heard that so often that, straight away, I answered back:

–Maybe he shouldn't have kicked me in the face.

And then what do you know, Scotty Haggis ups and slams the door.

–Some fucking police force, if that's the way you go on! I shouted out after him.

You know the way they always say – that when you get older, all the coppers start to look like babies.

& it's true of doctors too, I think. So half of the time, you just don't listen.

–He didn't kick you in the face, said Bravo, you're a liar.

Excellent, I thought, now she's every bit as bad as them.

And which was why I said, without thinking:

–Sgt Bravo?

–Yes? she says, kind of hopeful, leaning in.

As back in comes Davies and hands me a cigarette.

–You've got one more chance, he says, still livid.

& hands me a pen to write it all down.

You ought to have seen his face when he read it.

Gonks Go Beat in Glasgae! I had written.

Accompanied by a little picture of a haggis playing the bagpipes.

Then he hit me a dig – & after that I clammed up completely.

–The leopard never changes its spots, says Bravo.

For fuck's sake, Bravo – not you as well! I was thinking as they let me go back to my room.

Where *Desert Island Discs* was just finishing up on the wireless & the congregation were giving everything to the chorus of 'Lead Kindly Light' – the final request of today's guest, Harry Secombe.

With the chime of the bells and the warm swell of the organ taking me back straight away to those good old Sunday mornings that I remembered – when Alo and everyone else in the town was still alive, making their way up the hill to Mass.

–You'll soon be with us, I heard them say, and we're glad. Because whatever might have happened, we're proud of you – and will be always. Because Francie, son – you're a Brady. A son of ours who belongs to the town. This town, Francie, and no other.

And I have to admit that it made me feel – well, really quite wonderful.

With all of the tension and bitterness and anxiety that I'd felt while dealing with Haggis-Face: all of it had already ebbed away.

Not to mention talk about 'terminal'.

Which didn't seem to even exist as a word any more.

Or if it did, belonged in some world which bore no relation to that of *The Big Yaroo*, which was all about colour and happiness and possibility – just about as far as you could get from the grey and black-and-white misery of Dublin that night – and of which, as I'm sure you've gathered. I've been ashamed ever since it happened.

No matter what Bravo or Haggis-Face might say.

Or Clocker Kiernan, for that matter – wherever the fuck he ended up.

Give me Dr Cecil every time.

Not to mention poor old Lafferty and McGettigan, my unfortunate minders.

Yeah, that night had really 'done for them, mate' – as they used to say in the Edgar Wallace pictures.

So you can see why there mightn't be an awful lot left for me here in Fizzbag.

& which is why I've decided to bring the date of publication forward – & am going to have the first issue printed on the dot of 7 a.m. tomorrow morning.

Yes, ready and waiting for the whole world to inspect – all my potential readers!

Who shall then turn around to congratulate the editor – only to catch a glimpse of him, like the human Flash! – sailing on right out through the gates, already on his way to Paradise Island.

All aboard! he shouts – as he swipes the heads off dandelions with his stick.

And full-throating, good as any blackbird or swallow, pipes out his heart with his own personal Francie song of praise:

Easter bunny
Looking funny
With his basket of eggs
Bells are ringing
Children singing,
'Hooray for Easter Day!'

Look out, Paradise, here we come!

Because I'm afraid I just can't wait any longer, what with me being the fizziest old fizzbag in Fizzbag, chuckling away to myself as I gather up all my documents – thinking about Da and the two of us reading Korky – why, the cat of course, who was always on the front cover of *The Dandy*.

And who seemed to spend his time carving away in the middle of the pond – blue ice from which he cut the most perfect of dark round holes, so as to get himself a good substantial cache of fishies.

Except that, in this instance, now me and Da were sitting patiently in behind a bush, crouched there with our brand new deluxe telescope – where we'd been waiting all morning for a certain doctor as along he comes now with that big psychiatrist nose stuck into the middle of the paper, waddling along as only a hencum-human physician can.

& not seeing Korky's hole until it was too late, and – SPLASH! – right in goes the famous Clocker Kiernan as me & Da fall backwards into the bushes, with the two of us laughing until the pair of us are hoarse – & he keeps on walloping me with the rolled-up *Dandy*.

–*I once spent a week in Philadelphia*! you can hear him yelp as he makes more wild swings, with poor old Kiernan at the same time doing his best to climb up out of the hole – with two or three fish wriggling on top of his head.

–I think it was a Sunday! chuckles Da again – giving a sudden parp on his upraised bugle, as off goes The Clocker with his stupid head hanging down: *Bah! What a swiz!*

& which just goes to show you – that me and that old Da, whenever we wanted to – boy, could the two of us have ourselves a laugh.

Chapter 18

Throw Your Voice

So, as I was saying – here is, more or less, the final product – with only the 'Life of Grace' to go, which I'm delaying because what with it being the story most people, really, want to hear about, I've decided to reserve for the very front page.

With the photo that she gave me of herself and the Stripy-Tie Twins assuming pride of place – which, whatever about those two little fuckers, is the very least that she deserves, considering all her kindness to me.

There are still, unfortunately, quite a few misprints and smudges – but, hopefully, those can be forgiven.

Otherwise I really do think it looks splendid.

I've been up half the night working on it, so I hope so!

Not that there's a lot I can do about it – with my deadline looming, as I'm sure you can imagine.

Anyhow, see what you think …

```
THE BIG YAROO
Vol. 1, No. 1, 19 April
EDITORS & PUBLISHERS
Brady & Brady & Brady & Brady & Brady
EDITORIAL
Francis M. Brady (Director & Magazine
Editor)
```

Francis M. Brady (Deputy Editor)

F. Brady & F. Brady (Assistant Editors)

SALES

Frank Brady (Director)

Frank Brady (Condensed Books)

Frank Brady, F. Brady (Export)

Francis Brady (Gramophone Expert)

DEPARTMENTS

F. Brady (Publishing Projects)

F. Brady (Subscriber Services)

F. Brady (Market Research)

F. Brady (Education)

F. Brady (Office Administration)

ADVERTISING

Frank M. Brady (Director)

Frank M. Brady (Deputy)

F. Brady, F. Brady. F. Brady. F. Brady

SUBSCRIPTIONS

Rates, including postage. UK and Eire: 20
yo yos per annum (includes free gift)
Subscription Enquiries: F. Brady, Fizzbag
Mansions, Dundrum, Co. Dublin, Republic
of Ireland.

INTERNATIONAL EDITIONS OF THE BIG YAROO

Vice-President & General Manager:

Francis Brady

EXECUTIVE EDITOR

Frank Brady

I'll be glad to fill in a number of aspects of that unfortunate night
– because I know, in their hearts, that there are still a few things
about it that bother both Ronnie and Dr Cecil.

Which is understandable.

STOP PRESS: News coming in that The Professor has passed away.

Ah, poor old Big Brains – gone to join my old friend Uncle Alo. There'll soon be none of us left in Fizzbag.

–But at least he died peacefully, Mrs Beacon says, in his sleep.

–So he suffered no pain, she murmured, wringing her hands.

As off she went running, back up to her cottage – in order to keep an eye on her little pusscat Toddy Ray – who, by all accounts, isn't exactly doing the best either.

I only wish I could do more to help – but, as I was saying, I'm too busy getting ready for the off.

& boy, is it exciting – not only to have the magazine completed – but to have everything else ready, spot on perfect, in its place. I can't stop throwing glances at the panels – they really do look so sumptuous and colourful – just the way I remember *The Beezer* as a boy.

That's why I chose the broadsheet format – and many of the exact same ads.

Throw your Voice

```
Learn to throw your voice into trunks, behind
doors, everywhere. Instrument fits into your
mouth out of sight. Fool teachers, friends,
family. Free book: How to Be a Ventriloquist.
```

& I definitely will do that, throw my voice – before saying goodbye to Fizzbag forever.

Fire it here, there and everywhere, in fact – wherever the notion takes me. Not only about Grace and the conversations that we had, but also the day me and Mrs B headed once more for the James Connolly Memorial Hospital out in Blanchardstown, in the company of a brand-new minder who had taken the place of poor old Lafferty.

He had a little spud head and reminded me a bit of the piano-player Gilbert O'Sullivan.

–I never wanted to do this job, he says.

He was from Longford, he told us, and I had to laugh at the way he talked.

–*D'auld awspital*! he keeps on saying.

I mean – honest to God!

Potato head or not, I have to say he was a grand class of a fellow and I had plenty of laughs with him, about this and that.

Then, one day when we were coming through the gates, I leaned across the seat on my elbow and says:

–Do you know what they did to James Connolly in 1916? I says.

–No, he replies, and gives a shake of his spuddy wee head.

–*Shoh him in de faythe*! I says, and he goes all white.

I could see Mrs Beacon was even starting to laugh.

But old Gilbert in the end turned out to be one hundred per cent top class, I have to say – even joining in when I sang a couple of spirited snatches:

–*Every day's a holiday in Mr Moody's garden*!

–Frank, God love him, says Mrs Beacon, with all of her chins wobbling at once, he's always been fond of the music ha ha!

As up I looked up suddenly – and, hey presto, James Connolly and his amazing hospital wards!

As we sat in the foyer – and then, click click – along comes Miss Sandra Jones.

Smiling sweetly as she held on to her clipboard.

–This way, she says, and off we march.

With me still humming along with (Every day's a holiday in) 'Mr Moody's Garden' still hoping against hope that all the information in the X-rays would have somehow changed.

Which it hadn't, I'm afraid.

As a matter of fact, they told us without flinching, it would seem as if the disease has gotten worse.

Bah! was all you could think.

As I let out this roar and nearly frightened your man to death.

—Die, you sonsabitches dogs of Gonk!

To be honest, I think Mrs Beacon was mortally embarrassed – so, out of respect for her, I decided to button my lip.

As the minder starts on about inter-county football.

—Oh aye! They have a very good team this year! he says, about some crowd of monkey men I never heard tell of.

Then it was time for us all to go home.

Where Dr Cecil was waiting for us on the step – with this gizmo he'd got from America – talk about 'throw your voice!'

It was the whole new rage in therapy, he says, and wonderful results have been achieved.

—I'll see you later, says Mrs Beacon, as off she goes with your man, chatting away.

I was glad to see Gilbert had made a new friend – because with a spud head like that, they wouldn't exactly be queuing up.

***

It was all about verbalisation, Dr Cecil told me, giving vent to so many suppressed feelings.

—& Rodders McCork is the man here to help you do that, he said.

He was lifting the dummy out of the suitcase by its head – and propping it, splay-legged, up on the desk.

& I noticed it had the very same protruding lip & poseable arms as Troy, my favourite nautical puppet from Marineville.

In many respects he might have been his twin.

—This will go a long way to solving our problem, the doctor said, enabling you to vocalise things, which may even horrify you.

I have to say Dr Cecil could be eccentric.

As, without so much as another word, what does he do only sweep the figure up and plonk him down in the middle of my lap.

& what does Herr Doktor go and do then?

I honestly couldn't believe my ears! – begins to fire his voice around the room, the very same as your man on the back of *The Big Yaroo*.

Some people insist that there's something uncomfortable and kind of creepy about that particular type of doll.

Perhaps on account of their being approximately the same size as a normal schoolboy – to all intents and purpose a little miniature human.

Except that he isn't, in the strict sense, really what you could call 'alive'.

Because what he actually is, indisputably, is a shiny, blank-faced wooden doll.

One that is evidently lifeless – but at the same time, some-how, speaks and exudes a personality.

And while the reality is that what you're witnessing is two voices from a single source, the illusion is that one is watching two personalities sparring with one another.

But I personally think there is more to it than that – especially when they're wearing a red-and-white stripy school tie, exactly the same as the one my old friend Philip Nugent used to wear – like all of them did, in the school that he went to.

It makes me sad when I think about him now coming down the hill with his music case, all got up in his stripy tie and crested blazer.

Which I had actually tried on – one day when him and his family had all gone to the seaside for a picnic, and I had let myself into his house for a laugh.

I thought I looked good in that old stripy tie – but Philip didn't.

–*That's my tie*! you could hear him saying, as you pranced around his bedroom in front of the mirror, you have no business coming in here, helping yourself to peoples' property!

Oh now, it sure was a laugh – all the things you think about, going back them days.

The success of the Roderick McCorkindale Programme, Dr Cecil continued, had taken a lot of people by surprise. And all that it requires for the most wonderful of things to happen is that the patient give a specific degree of personal commitment and, in general, be enthusiastic about the programme and its methods.

With that old Cecil bashing away there along with Roddy, his hand up the back of his candy-striped jacket – just as he did on so many subsequent occasions.

With, after about fifteen or sixteen sessions, it becoming rewardingly evident that me and that old Rodders – we were getting along like a like a house on fire.

–Throw your voice!

–Not 'arf! I says, Doc.

& rabbited away with all sorts of old rubbish.

Including *What Would You Do?* and *Believe It or Not*!

Not that the doctor seemed to mind – for he was writing all of it down in a book.

I just couldn't wait to get in to have more chats – and it was all going good till he started quizzing me about Tom the Weaver.

I didn't like that.

A bit, maybe, yes – but not over and over, & not every time. Throw your voice?

–I'll throw fucking you Doc, I says, out the fucking window, so I will, right there.

& you want to see the face of poor old Dr Cecil.

Waugh! My programme has been a complete, useless failure.

–Not if you don't niggle me, I says.

But I suppose it proved that I wasn't over Tommy.

Maybe not over a lot of things – because when he came in that day and handed me the red pocket handkerchief just like Alo's – I had actually went and got sick all over him.

Roddy, I mean.

With Mrs Beacon having to clean it all up.

I can't remember *everything* about that day – but I think I must have had some kind of fit.

With all these voices, not just one, trying their best to push the others out of the way.

But it was a horrible feeling – not something you'd want to happen again.

With the strangest thing being – that, out of the corner of my eye, it was as if I could see the dummy there looking at me.

Like he was saying: I can do this any time. Make you throw your voice.

Make you even fuck yourself out the window, if I want to.

Throw your voice?

Just you remember and be careful, my friend – for it's me who does the throwing around here.

& then when I went to challenge him on it – he was just a stupid dummy.

Yes, that was all he seemed to be – not even a proper doll.

Just lying there, blank-eyed, with one arm hanging down.

Chapter 19

Pansy Potter
the Strongman's Daughter

The greatest thing about being the editor of your own magazine is that you can write what you like, at any time you want, and there won't be anyone saying I won't allow that, and take out big lumps of it without even bothering to ask your permission. & most of the time not knowing that they could be the most important things for you – probably having kept you awake all night.

Which was more or less the case last night – not long after I'd closed my eyes, and found Da appearing right there in front of me, looking no more than thirty years of age & wielding his trumpet like the proudest man in town.

As he took me by the hand and, without as much as a by your leave, led me briskly straight into the kitchen – to show me how the radio had been transformed into the tiniest glowing theatre, complete with little frilled curtains tied up across its glass panel front, as the English compère proudly called our name:

–Yes! Here they are – the ones we've been waiting for all evening, ladies and gentlemen. Welcome to The London Palladium!'

Where, it turned out, they were recording another instalment of *Sing Something Simple* – only now with him as the star, our humble little kitchen having turned itself into a stage – as he marched around and high-kicked his legs, parping away for all he was worth, with that great big belly stuck out in front, and his eyes full of fire the likes of which you'd never seen.

–Oh yes, old Duffy thinks his circus is the tops, but he hasn't reckoned on Benny Brady's marching band of troupers!

Before suddenly turning and facing into the wings – and, with an uncharacteristically flamboyant flourish, calling out with a yelp:

–Ladies and gentlemen, I give you Eddie Calvert, the man with the golden trumpet!

As the Brylcreemed star of the 1950s arrived onstage with a glinting, golden-toothed smile, and the pair of them commenced blasting those shiny twin bugles for all the world like dreamy lonesome bullfighters.

–*Oh mein Papa*, to me you were so wonderful.

As Da looked at me – I was sitting in the front – his eyes crinkling up at the corners the way they did.

–Sometime, son, in another world, I heard him muse softly.

It's like the more you tend to write about things, the more stuff comes up that you really do not expect.

With tears of what I can only describe as something very near joy appearing in my eyes only a half an hour or so ago as I dragged two butterflies across with the mouse and inserted them in the middle of the two zeros at the latter end of the title name.

& all I can say is that I hope Tommy approves of my choice – a greenish cabbage white & a rainbow-hued painted lady – because it's him they're in honour of, and those once-upon-a-time, end-of-summer Brixton days.

'Those Elusive Butterfly Days', I have called the article – written up in honour of his son.

Which I never believed he'd had, until that day.

& about whom he had never so much as said a single thing, not in all the time I'd known him.

But there you go – there he was on the terrace, all those many long days ago now, standing with his mother out among the parked cars.

Although, strictly speaking, it wasn't any of my business – but, having always thought of Tommy as a brother, I suppose I couldn't have helped myself even if I'd tried.

So off I went, around by the back of the kitchens, nipping in behind a big laurel tree to earwig.

Initially I had taken the roundy woman to be his sister – because never in a million years could you have imagined her to be Junie Moon.

No, not a chance – more like the type that you'd see in Tesco's, with a great big padded anorak and a bit of an old crocheted beanie perched on top of her head, like Pansy Potter the Strongman's Daughter.

& I have to say that she didn't look well.

Not that I was anyone to talk, for in recent times my own old phizog – it had turned the colour of turnips so it had – thanks to the efforts of Dr Gonk and Co.

It was deeply frustrating trying to hear what they were saying, and by the time they were finished I was as bad as The Professor – with a pile of laurel leaves having stacked up around my feet.

Yes, it sure was a long way from Brixton, they kept saying, from those days in the beer garden when they'd sit around talking about Led Zeppelin and Procol Harum, and then cycle off up to Hampstead for a picnic – watching painted ladies and cabbage whites performing great big elaborate minuets high above the clear rippling skin of the ponds. & it was sad that all of that was gone, for sure, I thought – but even if it was, at least he had lived it, and had the good nature & generosity to share it all with me.

Something which I admired and will always look up to –
even if he sometimes wandered off into a hippy dippy daze and
you weren't, maybe, sure if he was making the whole thing up.

As he sat there in the pump shed waving his cigarette, pushing
back that long matted curtain of hair, describing the butter-yel-
low sunshine of the garden – where they all lay back in their blue
jeans and Indian shirts, with wisps of woodsmoke coming drifting across the fence.

–In Held 'Twas in I, I remember him saying, In Held 'Twas
in I, man – yeah?

Whatever the fuck that was supposed to mean – as he tapped
the fag and stared right at you, like he was expecting some equally
big brainbox statement from you.

& which could be frustrating, seeing as I didn't have the first
faintest clue of what the devil he was on about – & sometimes, I
admit, it could really get on my nerves.

But I'll tell you this – if it did, well then I'm glad of it –
because when it comes to the Weavers, Tommy 'The Hippy', as
they called him – no matter how he disgraced them or how much
junk he ended up pumping into his arm, he was a complete and
utter gentleman when compared to that snout-faced bastard of a
greyhound he had for a brother.

& who I hear has recently been involved in some embezzle-
ment scandal to do with the council – & is in serious danger of
losing his job.

& has gone back crazy on the drink as a result.

& is probably, right at this very moment, propping up the
bar counter in some godforsaken border town – blaming his
misfortune on what had happened that day in the churchyard at
Mount Argus – when he had come within a 'hair's breadth' blah
blah of nearly being killed.

Yes, off we go again with Denny Weaver – and the same old tale about that severed fucking brake cable, and how the car had suddenly given out.

As – *smash*! – in he goes to the wall and bangs his head.

An event which, of course, I'd rather had never happened. With the lot of us, looking back on it, being under enough stress in that church, without having to endure any more. The Professor, in particular, was in a very bad way.

–Poor old Tommy, I remember Big Brains saying, shuffling away from one foot to the other as he used my shoulder to steady himself – and then, after coughing like a hurricane, creating twice as much commotion in his efforts to locate his hankie.

Which he eventually found – with my assistance.

And that, I'm happy to say, calmed him down – but did nothing for me, I regret to admit – because all the way through the service, no matter how I tried I just couldn't keep from looking up towards the front where Denny Weaver and those fucking accusing eyes of his kept turning – you know who he is, don't you, they said – and you know what it is that he done.

With it all, eventually, coming to a head.

When he curled that lip and shook his head wearyingly.

As if to say: there's nothing can be done.

Because, I mean – who's he to say that?

Yes, who is he to go and fucking say the like of that?

Then, worst of all, his friend turned around.

–You don't think we know? Oh we know everything – and, indeed, a lot more than ever made the papers.

I went white, I swear to God. I could feel it.

Because it was as if they were just cruelly trying to provoke and manipulate me – like they wanted or needed some form of public declaration – perhaps on account of their grief over Tommy, I don't know.

& that I could understand – knowing how bad, in our own way, we were feeling.

But the manner in which it was all being executed – I can't tell you how clever it was.

Oh, extremely so.

Because no one, you see, could accuse him directly.

All I can say is that it made me sad. As I tried to calm down.

But then I heard him – clear as a bell, cupping his hand around his mouth.

–I mean, it's one thing to have a row with neighbours – but to break in and butcher someone like a pig. It's just a pity that they ended capital punishment.

& that was what did it.

Like they say on the cover of *Boys' World* – when you sit down and spend some time considering it – given such circumstances: *What would you do?*

***

–I've never felt so lonely in my life, said Tommy, after she'd left, so lonesome and ashamed.

–I know what you mean, Tommy, I'd replied.

Having felt the same after my mother and the rats. But I suppose that's the way, and all we can do is go back to our work.

**'The Big Yaroo (The Truth in the News)'
Including today's special feature:
'My Most Unforgettable Character',
starring Laurence Muggivan,
alias 'The Big Brains Prof'**

who was coming down Madison Avenue with his fiancée when she suddenly announced it was time to go into Macy's.

So in they went to buy a bottle of perfume as the old Big Brains Prof, he sat by the counter and thought about nothing, only how lucky he was — not only to be engaged to be married but to be a supporter of the best and most celebrated football team in all Ireland, who were almost certain to bring home the All-Ireland trophy.

So preoccupied was he that he didn't even notice his girlfriend buying gloves — delicate ones in cheeky black lace.

In fact, so excited was The Professor that, in his imagination, he was actually taking part in the game.

Delivering an almighty wallop of a kick to the centre of the leather ball, as his wife-to-be applauded wildly on the terraces.

'My husband is King of Ireland!' he heard her cry as he drove the ball fiercely into the back of the net.

'Favourite Hurling Tournaments: Fr Ron Remembers'

I was in the process of finishing off this particular article, which I'd been up all night polishing and researching – because, as I'm sure you've gathered, hurling is a subject that I happen to know sweet fuck all about, when I heard something moving stealthily around outside, and pushed back my chair to find Corrigan the nosey bastard, brazen as brass staring in the window.

–Oh! You're the boy! he says, and sniggers, oh, you would have to be the man for sure. Oh yes, I know about you. Make no mistake, The Scuttler's wise to it all alright!

I swiped off my eyeshade and went straight away over to confront the long-nosed wretch.

–Take a hike, Corrigan! I said, or can't you see that I'm busy?

Then he looked right through me – I have to admit, it did make me uneasy.

–Your time around here is done, my friend, so be mindful of what The Scuttler says.

& when I looked again, him and his barrow were gone.

& I turned to see Ricky Shabs in his shell suit – lying across the armchair like he's been appointed deputy editor.

–What's the show, bro'? he says, and sets about skinning a roll-up.

Apparently they've discovered all these mummies in the Guatemalan desert, he tells me.

–Wearing Adidas trainers, you can put that in your magazine, he says.

And I had to laugh – and was glad to, after Corrigan.

–You got to be kidding, Ricks, I say. But no.

–This is really serious, Old School! he says, because ordinary mummies, they don't wear trainers.

A closer inspection of his phone revealed that the figures were indeed wearing sports shoes – corpses unearthed from 3000 BC.

&, although we kept on laughing, I just couldn't get The Scuttler out of my mind.

Had he seen me, I wondered.

Then Ricky Shabs said he wanted to use the computer.

Talking away about this film that he had 'in prep'.

–*The Sandman*, it's called, about these rogue CIA operatives who run a deep-cover syndicate called The Boys.

Kind of like *The Assassination Bureau*, long ago, I suggested, huh?

But he wasn't listening to a word I said.

–Come on now Ricky, I have things to do! I told him.

& then what's he do?

Gets up and shouts at me:

–*Racist!*

Before slamming the door and away out across the grass.

But I'm going to leave him a note as well – along with the article: 'Ricky Shabs Remembers'.

& I think that'll please him.

But right now it's time to tie up these bags and get everything ready for the race of a lifetime – to get off to Portrane and soak up the loveliest sunrise-yellow Easter sun of all time!

Boy, are my old pals going to be surprised and excited – when they look out the window and see me coming coasting along the road.

–Glory be to Jaysus if it isn't Francie Brady! I thought he said he was never leaving Fizzbag!

But that's the world, though, ain't it fellers?

Filled with all sorts of unexpected surprises.

& isn't that, after all, what makes life worth living?

Unless, that is, it happened to be of the sort that poor old Big Brains' girlfriend discovered – when she came into his bed in the middle of the night and in the process released a monster, who not only ignored her for the rest of her life but actually drove her into a mental hospital, along with the assistance of his parish priest – I mean, did you ever?

Or maybe the one Scuttler Corrigan has in mind – to spoil what promises to be the most glorious day in my entire life.

The Easter-Wrecker is his new name now.

But he won't, you see – he fucking won't!

Because I've been through way too much to permit, at this point, any form of discouragement.

With my bags all packed and the angel of Dresden ready to guide me.

So, screw you Scuttler – this Easter is all mine!

With only one more sleep in total to go – oh Jesus!

I'm so excited, I can just about contain it, I said to Troy.

Awkwardly hauling him out by his foot.

With the three of us just lying there dozing for a while beside the computer – until I came to again and noticed that the light outside had begun to fail – and did some exercises to slow down my accelerating heart.

–I just can't believe it's tomorrow, I said to The Captain – all choked up when I said it, to be honest, it really is hard to get my head around it.

–I know, I heard him reply, but you must remember that, whatever way it might be affecting you, what you are facing into is, in all likelihood, the most exciting and wonderful day you have experienced in your life. One, which will be spoken of for generations to come – by people, most likely, who are not yet even born! Now isn't that something?

And I had to agree that, yes it definitely was.

–*Anything can happen in the next half hour!* I squealed, suddenly grabbing a hold of him – and giving him such a hug that, I swear to God, I nearly snapped the wee fucker in half!

Oh now.

Now what have I left to put in before I go.

Ah yes – old Rodders, that's what it is.

Roddy & The Stripies.

Brr – even the very slightest thought gives me the creeps.

I couldn't believe it when I woke up in the middle of the night – because I'd really been exhausted, working all day on the magazine. & it could have been because I'd been researching pieces on horror – having gone through thirty or forty publications.

If this one doesn't send a shiver down your spine, one of them read, you may well be a sociopath.

Well, whether that's true or not, all I can remember is hearing this fizzing sound, which stopped for a while and then started up again – only, this time, louder.

As I threw back the covers and felt the most awful dread beginning to overwhelm me.

& perspiration breaking in heavy drops across my forehead.

Then – the very same noise again – I could make out something at the bottom of the dormitory, followed by the sound of low, suppressed laughter.

Before realising – I almost laughed out loud when it dawned on me – that it was nothing more than the spitting of a malfunctioning strip light located on the landing directly outside the door.

And, although I mightn't have been laughing out loud – I was, in fact, laughing.

& that was when I saw the figure – standing motionless at the other end of the room – just observing me.

Watching me keenly, not moving a muscle.

Before it began to move slowly in my direction – with the sound of each footstep seeming to mimic the steady, slow rhythm of my heart.

–Hi, said Roddy.

Except it wasn't Roddy McCorkindale, was it.

–Hi, it said again.

Now it was standing right beside my bed.

–I want you to meet my brother, it whispered.

As I looked up and saw his identical twin.

–This is Alan, I was told, & I'm Ivor.

–Alan, said one.

–Ivor, said the other.

–We believe you may know our grandmother.

–Our lovely grandmother, whose name is Grace.

–You broke into her shop, didn't you Francis?

–You're a bad man, Brady, so we've come for retribution.

–Touch her, did you – was that what you did?

–Was that the reason?

I felt like sobbing, it was just so wrong.

–Now you'll have to pay, they said.

When I looked again, the two of them were gone.

& there was nothing but the half-open window and the blind, with its toggle rattling against the glass.

But it didn't happen, did it – because that old Frank, in the end, he outwitted the bastards.

Just as he will that snooping, scuttling Corrigan – who has nothing other to do than pry into people's lives. As I tie up my bags and get ready with my 3-In-One Oil, if you please!

& making sure to consult my special *Beano Annual* – containing, as it does, one's indispensable inventory of instructions, including:

1. Replace worn brakes immediately.
2. Oil your machine often but sparingly.
3. Check that your reflector is clean and properly angled.
4. Tighten fig. A to avoid wheel shake.

–Look out, suckers! I cheer as I punch the air, yep, look out *señores* 'cos here he comes – Frank Brady, the one and only human Flash! Yee-haw, *kemo sabe*! Lambay Island, here we come! For nothing can stop the Brady boy now!

With only two more *Yaroo* pages to edit!

So, get your subscriptions ready, folks – as that final deadline comes drawing near, yee-haw!

Easter bunny
Looking funny
With his basket of eggs
Bells are ringing
Children singing,
'Hooray for Easter Day!'

Chapter 20
The Big Breakout

As through those electronic gates I'll come flying, perched on top of Madame La Road Runner, the one and only Queen of Wheeltown – zipping along that old highway towards Lambay like the greatest racer ever seen in the Tour de France.

With it being like, overnight, you've somehow gone and grown yourself a set of the sturdiest wings.

As hordes of flag-waving imaginary crowds swell to bursting point along the roadsides and sidewalks – for the purpose of cheering their hero along, yes, their own personal one-man, indomitable Flying Machine.

Like a living streak of silver mercury, scarcely visible to the poor old human eye with tears of pride flowing down your cheeks – what with all those faces of the dead lined up along the pavement.

–Hooray for the Tour of the Departed! shouts my uncle Alo, waving his little red hankie above his head.

–I don't think I've ever been so content, I said to Troy, flicking for the last time through my pages.

With the lot of us there – standing, in full colour, on the white sand of Paradise Island, as The Professor and Uncle Alo just carry on chatting away beside a giant statue.

–How do you suppose they fashioned such extraordinary structures? wonders The Professor, shading his eyes. Because, after all, Francie, I hear him saying to me, I'm well over six foot two and beside this statue I seem like a dwarf. Mysterious, isn't it?

–It certainly is, I agreed, Professor Big Brains, worse than Jack Palance's *Believe It or Not!*

He nodded and knitted his brow, once again considering the breathtaking enormity of the grey quartz figure, casting its shadow across an infinite blanket of sand, set against a cobalt blue sky.

–Do you know what it reminds me of? he continued, a certain unforgivable action of my own – perpetrated many years ago now – an act, which saw our Creator turn His face away. When I traduced my fiancée, shamefully. I wanted to die.

He was addressing the stone carving more than me.

–& there is nothing more terrible in this mortal world than the realisation that the one who has made you has elected, forever, to avert His gaze.

I had to put it down.

Because I couldn't read any more.

–It's the loneliest feeling in the universe, he said.

But then I knew that, didn't I?

As The Professor started laughing hysterically – & when I turned the page, he was bidding me goodbye.

–Don't worry, Frank, for we'll be seeing you soon. & I just can't tell you how much we are all looking forward to that.

–Thanks for everything, son, he said.

& was gone.

So that's, more or less, everything taken care of, I said, as I packed away my first copy of the magazine and left the digital image on the screen where I knew Ron would see it.

With it being the last thing I expected, the night before my life's most important day.

It was horrible – so awful. What was to, eventually, happen.

Now, of all times – that was all I could think.

As I looked along the bottom of the line of lockers – and knew, straight away, that I hadn't imagined it.

–Surprise! Surprise! It's the Stripy-Tie Twins!

–He really did think he could get out of it, I heard one of them whisper.

Stepping from out behind the lockers – sighing softly as he stared directly at me.

I slowly began raising my head under the covers – only then realising that it wasn't Alan or Ivor. But someone else.

Yes, Philip Nugent – the schoolfriend whose mother I'd murdered – horribly.

Except it hadn't ever been meant to happen.

–But then, you always say that, I heard Philip Nugent whisper.

He was wearing his belted brown gaberdine coat.

When I looked again, I saw that he was gone.

With nothing remaining but the pale coin of the moon.

Or was it the sun.

–I don't know! I heard myself cry out loud, but I'm not waiting around to find out – because, for once and for all, I'm getting out of here!

& which I am going to do now – right this very minute, and leave those memories far behind – both of Philip and 'The Lonely Widow'.

Which is funny when you think about it – for, what with all the people who used to be in and out of her shop every minute, Grace was just about the furthest thing you could imagine from lonely.

No matter what the papers said – stupid fucking tabloids, it was even worse than the first time – with Philip's mother, I mean, when I actually *had* been guilty of something.

Because I hadn't meant to hit anyone that night – especially not a Russian who turned out not to be even a Russian!

They have my heart broke thinking about them so they have.

But at least they have taught me something – that whenever you're pitting yourself against the forces of law and order, for the love of fuck leave nothing to chance.

Because, as I was just saying to Troy, that – always and ever – has been my undoing.

Except this time around – my planning has been out of this world.

With even the magazine devoid of any mistakes – I know, for I checked it again just now.

I'm up and down like a yo-yo to the office – passing time until zero hour dawns.

Here on this bright, crisp Easter Sunday morning – with Fr Ron still fiddling around up there.

I wish to fuck he'd go and let me get on with it.

As I administer to old 'Madame' yet another squirt of ye olde trusty 3-In-One.

What a gleaming model she has turned out to be!

Just the perfect machine for the Tour of the Faithful Departed!

So come on Ronsers, hurry yourself up, will you Father?

Already I can see his great big Baby Crockett eyes when he discovers the cover of *The Big Yaroo* sitting waiting for him there on the screen.

Dedicated to 'My old buddy, Fr Ron'.

As I open the bag and check on Troy – who is in there, sound, with not a bother on him at all.

–*Anything can happen in the next half-hour*! I laugh.

As he smiles in recognition and I zip up the pannier.

& which is not a little amusing in itself because we've already agreed that many people think that there's something odd about ventriloquists' dummies – & Troy Tempest he definitely looks like one.

But there is absolutely nothing threatening about him.

How could there be?

Otherwise why would I be able to bring him to bed with me every night?

Something, which I've been doing now for quite some time – although I didn't ever dare mention the fact to Cecil.

Because I know he'd probably just go and make a big thing of it, & start pestering me with all these questions.

So whatever relationship might have evolved – it's strictly between The Captain and myself.

Because there isn't anything you can't say to him – really.

& I mean anything!

–I'm sorry, Philip! I said to him last night, about what happened to your mother!

& all Troy does is just lie there, and listen.

Like a dummy, yes – but you know that he understands.

&, like Cecil says, is helping you to find a way to.

So that's great.

& why the three of us are all ready to get rolling – Troy & me and ye olde angel of Dresden.

–Anything can happen in the next half hour! I yelped, grabbing a hold of him – and giving him such a hug that, I swear to God, I nearly snapped him again!

As, what do you know – don't I hear this lovely little Alpine horn – yes, the little German shepherdess and her piping away goodo.

–Good man Frank, you're the boy that will show them, eh?

As she begins to sing, so sweetly I can't tell you:

Easter bunny
Looking funny
With his basket of eggs

When her voice being so lovely that it was almost the very same as being in a state of grace, the way you'd have been on a Saturday night after confession.

& which was why I went down to the pump house to say goodbye, and maybe recite a wee small prayer.

In memory of Tommy and all the good times we'd once shared there.

Closing the heavy doors behind me, as I lay there sprawled on a great big mound of slack, sucking my thumb.

Considering my achievements – with the magazine and everything – and my forthcoming Great Escape of All Time.

Which is now imminent.

But then I heard it – the sharp sound of a breaking twig.

–Who's there? I called out.

No reply, so I said it again.

–Did you hear me? I said.

Again, nothing.

Then I heard another muffled noise around the back – and, again, seeing nothing, my heart nearly gave out in my chest when I came back to find The Scuttler standing there waiting in the doorway with his barrow.

–Oh you're some boy alright, he hissed, yes you are the trickster. But then, Brady, you always were.

I didn't reply – just stood in silence as his gaze went through me.

–Aye, you'd be the right class of an operator alright – trying to pull the wool over people's eyes.

Before stepping into the light, running his tongue along his thin lower lip as he tugged the peak of his flat cap forward.

In the quiet of the dawn you could hear his even breathing.

–I've got one or two questions I'd like to ask, he said.

–Questions? I replied, playing absently with my oily rag. The one I'd been using to clean Her Majesty.

—Aye, that'd be it, he continued, measuredly, maybe you'd like to tell me what you were doing in the orchard this morning?

—Orchard? I said, my cheeks beginning to burn.

—Yes. That's what I said. Perhaps you'd like to explain what it was you were doing with that big bag of papers?

—Papers? I said, doing the best I could to make light of it.

But with the truth being that he had taken me completely by surprise.

—You were seen burning papers in the orchard, he said quietly, hauling them across the grass in a big black sack.

—Big black sack? I croaked.

—Aye. A big plastic refuse bag.

—No, I said, I'm afraid I have to say you're mistaken.

—Oh, he smiled, mistaken, is it?

—Yes. That's right, I replied, I'm sorry to have to say that you are somewhat erroneous in your assumption, Mr Corrigan.

—Erroneous, eh? That's a big word. Like one that maybe you'd see on a fellow's computer. When he's not looking at bad women.

—Bad women? I said, what a laugh. I don't know where you get your information from.

But brazen as I sounded, my face and neck were now a deep shade of crimson.

—I'm the editor of a magazine, I explained, a magazine called *The Big Yaroo*.

—Yes, you are, he smiled, I know that. And another thing I know is that that's not the name of it.

—Oh is it not, I said, well seeing as you know so much, what then is the name of it?

—*Readers' Wives* it's called! That'd be the name of it, I'd be thinking. The name of your famous publication – *Readers' Wives*. Or *Tits Monthly*, if you like. So I suppose you must be quite an authority on them now. Are you, Frank?

After saying that, he was lucky he didn't end up going the same as Mr Denny Weaver.

Because he really did annoy me.

But, just at that moment, Betty Spaghetti happened to be passing – reciting the alphabet backways as she began emptying prayer cards and rosaries onto the gravel & saying they were planning to have a little service for the Professor.

–Yes! she said, a wee bit of a Mass, so will you help me maybe pick one out?

I don't know how many Sacred Hearts and Maria Gorettis she dug out from the bottom of her handbag.

As I elbowed Corrigan out of the way and let Betty accompany me back to the office.

Where I found her a lovely little picture of The Prof – one that he'd given me himself, standing on the observation deck in Dublin airport, laughing and waving that day in 1947.

Spaghetti liked it so much that she said she was honoured to accept it – and had actually offered me a small sum of money.

Which I politely declined.

But by now I was becoming agitated, still thinking about Corrigan and his breathtaking impertinence.

Yes – all I could think was, just who the hell does The Scuttler think he is?

& the more I thought, the more livid I became.

So that was why I went over to Ricky – because I knew he had his number on his phone.

I didn't say who I was but told him I had a proposition I'd like to put to him – one which he might find to his benefit.

Involving a substantial sum of money, which, being a notorious skinflint, I knew he wouldn't resist.

& I was right – as I remained behind the linden, watching him strutting like a bantam cock, whistling.

Then I was away.

–I hear you're fond of sacks, I said, coming up behind him, then let's see then how you like this one!

He said he couldn't breathe, flailing & kicking as I pulled it over his head.

Before dragging him into the back of the shed and trussing him up in behind the boiler. Talk about yaroos!

You never heard anything like it.

But, hopefully, that will put manners on him, I thought.

As I dusted myself down and went back up towards the main building.

–*Mmph! Mmph!* was all you could hear.

Sometimes you have to take these measures – whether it's something you want to do or not.

Oh man, it's a laugh! I was saying, as I look over and see Ricky coming across with chips.

–So, bro', what's happenin'? he says, chomping away as he offers me the bag.

–Oh, nothing much, I says, and then he says he's sorry for having called me racist.

He's a great old skin, the Ricks, all in all – & if there's anyone I'm going to miss, it would have to be him.

He wanted me to play a game of snooker but already, in my mind, I was back inside my room.

I don't think, in my life, that I've ever felt so free.

I mean – one minute you're tramping across old wet playing fields or trudging abandoned refectory corridors, then the next thing you're off on a bike to your own private island, laughing away about that stupid old stripy-tie pair of dummies.

Which – I couldn't believe it! – had actually terrified me the very first time they came, accusing me of all these things.

& it really did seem as if they meant it, irrespective of whether or not any of it was true.

One of them had actually spat in my face.

As the other leaned across and looked at me with those swivelling eyeballs.

–Make some small little gesture of restitution, he demanded.

–For what you done, hissed Ivor.

–Did, corrected Alan, for what it is he did.

–Yes, nodded Ivor, for what it is you did.

–We're truly sorry, his twin brother continued, that events have come to this, Brady Pig – but we really feel we have explored every possible alternative.

–And have decided, ultimately, that we really have no choice.

Then he plunged the blade – availing of the smaller wing, the one normally used for cutting tobacco – pushing it right into the centre of my eye.

I'd screamed at the time – I mean what else could you do.

–So, come along, Brady, be a good chap and say: I'm a rubbish old pig!

–I'm rubbish, I said, a rubbish old pig!

–Because I've always been rubbish, continued Stripy-Tie Alan.

–Because I've always been rubbish.

–Ever since the day I was conceived in my mother's womb.

–Ever since the day I was conceived in my mother's womb.

–Before being wrenched!

–Before being wrenched!

–And given the opportunity to breathe God's good clean air!

–And given the opportunity to breathe God's good clean air!

–Something which I didn't deserve!

–Something which I didn't deserve!

–An opportunity which I most certainly didn't merit!

–An opportunity which I most certainly didn't merit!

–Just like the one I'm being generously offered now.

–Just like the one I'm being generously offered now, I said.

–To end my life by my own miserable hand!

–To end my life by my own miserable hand!

They wanted me to kill myself – but no Sir, I'm afraid. Not Frank Brady.

As I heard Troy chuckle – just a little tinkle.

–No, Captain Tempest – in the end I managed to outsmart those rotters. And now they'll never get near me again.

–Man dear! laughed Troy, boy will they be raging!

–They certainly will, interjected the little angel, barely audible from the bottom of the bag.

Man alive, such times! I thought.

With it only now beginning to dawn – just how well things had seemed to turn out in the end.

In spite of so many frustrations over the years – not least among them my original, embarrassing attempt at escape – and those now-laughable subsequent events in Grace's.

Which I couldn't have possibly ever foreseen – when I so innocently admitted myself into her home.

She'd been left the shop by an elderly grand-aunt – well-to-do gentry, solid old-time Protestant stock.

Laydee De Courcey-Meers, if you puh-lease!

Although what the fuck she was doing in Gardiner Street – looking after the likes of Mickser and his hoodie junk-chomping pals is beyond me, the worst street in Western Europe.

But once you got in, it really was special – not like an ordinary charity shop at all.

One's golden kingdom of Enable Ireland – that was how I thought of it at the time.

215

&, in many ways still do – it's just a pity that I'd selected the night when the whole Western world seemed under attack.

& with the streets of Dublin city being filled from top to bottom with cops and patrol cars, searching everywhere for me – &, I suppose, Arabs.

So, unlike now, I'm afraid Frank Brady, you couldn't have timed your jailbreak worse.

After I escaped from my minders – or, rather, just not arriving back with their bets – all I can remember is pushing up the cover of the manhole – and looking up and down to make sure that the coast was clear, in the process nearly getting flattened by a speeding furniture van.

So anyway, right back down I goes again – Frank Brady. Biding his time as he waits for another chance.

& then, after ten or fifteen minutes had passed, pushing ye old manhole cover up again, and away off down the street like the clappers.

Where The Case of the Lonely Widow was about to begin.

Although what time it was exactly when I found myself standing outside Grace's wonderland – to this day I couldn't honestly say, not with any degree of accuracy.

But it has to have been somewhere between two and three in the morning.

Do you know what I always used to think about charity shops?

That all there's ever in them is clothes belonging to the dead.

But that wasn't going to stop me now, I thought, as I shinned up this great big oak to the side of the building and climbed across the fence that bordered Grace's garden, using the Swiss Army knife to hack my way through all the bushes and undergrowth and briars.

With nothing but the sound of wailing sirens to be heard across the city – whether from ambulances or police cars I couldn't say – like they were doing their best to out-perform New York, who were over there watching their citizens turning into coal dust right in front of them.

As I stood there, rigid, outside her back door, with the hairs bristling on the back of my neck.

One thing, looking back, that I would have to say about the so-called break-in was just how simple and hopelessly uncomplicated it actually was when it came to gaining access.

A deft little flick of the small blade and I was in.

Hey presto! yes, there I was – inside Madame La Courtney's own personal private basement.

Her very own noble Wonderland of Dreams.

With it all laid out in front of me as I struck a match – the first thing I laid eyes on was the ornate portrait of her twin grand-sons – as if to say look who's here, well well.

It was like a toyshop for adults – everything you've ever dreamed of owning – right there in front of your eyes.

Comics, board games – assorted military uniforms.

& a great big stack of old photograph albums.

So quiet and peaceful did it seem that I felt delirious.

There was even an old-fashioned wingback armchair – just sitting there in shadow – like Francie Brady's own private throne.

So I wasn't going to disappoint it.

–Hello there, Miss Grace Courtney's Cave of Wonders – it really is nice to make your acquaintance, I said.

As I reached in my pocket to find a little pill, one of the ones that I'd lifted off McGettigan – & which wasn't long in taking effect.

So I have to say that it really felt good – just sitting relaxing there on my personal throne – because I have to admit I was tired after my exertions.

With my toes mellowing into the softest of warm sponge – as a wave of contentment broke across me in a sigh of peace.

This was a great place for your holidays, I thought, Grace Courtney's B&B.

With the little Gonks in my head gone upstairs to put on their jammies.

Exactly how powerful that tablet had been, I don't think I could really say – all I know is that, when I opened my eyes again, what did I see?

Only the twins – looking at me from a photograph and laughing hysterically as they spoke my name.

They looked so funny, I remember thinking, in their caps and blazers exactly like Philip's.

With Ivor then, astonishingly, emerging right out of the picture and standing in front of me shaking his head as he said:

–I'm terribly sorry, but this really isn't quite cricket, you know!

Then I looked around, and there was his brother – standing directly opposite – with the framed gilt portrait now completely blank.

Ivor moaned as he pushed back his cap.

–Look here! he said, just what is the meaning of this? You going and breaking into our nana's shop?

–Yes, Francis Brady – please be quick and explain yourself!

As I struck a match and began to stutter – doing my best to come up with an explanation, before receiving an almighty belt of a crowbar across the face.

With two other bastards, like bears, standing now in front of me – glowering & snarling – you never seen the like of it.

& I have to apologise for previously calling them Russians – because I'm perfectly aware now that they weren't any such thing, no Sir.

& I'd better not say they're Romanians either – because, like with Ricky Shabs, that would probably turn out to be racist.

But I will say this – whatever part of Eastern Europe they were from, they sure did breed them good down there.

Built like a fucking brick shithouse, this fellow was.

& now here he was, coming right at me again.

Wielding the crowbar and spouting all this Russian – sorry, not Russian.

All this Eastern European talk anyway – and, which when translated, means or less the same thing:

–Let's get stuck in & batter Francie Brady!

Well, like I told them – they were welcome to try.

They were originally from Romania and Estonia, it later transpired, with the remainder comprising a well-organised Dublin criminal gang who specialised in the theft of second-hand goods, and coming from no further than five minutes away, down the road in Summerhill if you don't mind. But now they'd had it.

As I prepared at last to make my move – with Tattoo-Head frantically firing shirts and shoes into a bag.

–*Tatal tau avea alti copii urate*? I heard Tattoo laughing, all delighted as he made these jokes, blabbing away down a mobile phone about the night of the Twin Towers presenting a fine opportunity to stage a robbery.

Before snapping it shut and whistling away, without so much as a bother on him – before he got a good hardy smash of a statue across the head.

–Take that! I said, swinging the alabaster sculpture, a maiden with her mouth hanging open, fountain-style – hitting Tattoo first and then Buzzcut.

You ought to have heard their miserable yelps!

–Where are your fucking rockets now, you dogs, I said, and was feeling real good.

Not that I was home and dried – far from it.

For did that old Buzzcut get his revenge or what.

With a whole fucking tribe of them appearing then from nowhere, descending on top of me and scything away for all they were worth – like a pack of slavering Nazi Dobermans, if that's not racist.

With Tattoo's great big toecap landing on my head & the woman who was with them sitting on top of my fucking chest.

Someone's chest – I mean, can you believe it?

With me, I'm afraid, being so far gone, with the tab and everything, that all I could think of was W.C. Fields.

& Da waltzing around in his old-time baggy brown suit.

–*It's that man again!* I could hear him say, that lad of ours – I'm afraid he's up to his tricks again!

As the woman's six-inch heel went right into my eye, and all I could see after that was my father saying:

–Hush now.

Before Juliet Bravo and the Old Bill arrived with their sirens screaming and caught the whole lot of us – hands-down – in the act.

With the woman turning out to be the worst of the lot in the end, bawling and crying and insisting it was me who had ripped her shirt, and saying in the court she was still finding bits of glass in her arm,

& not so much a word about the heel she had shoved in my face.

But there you have it – that's the way the cookie crumbles, I suppose – with all the little Gonks asleep in their beds, and the whole of Eastern Europe deciding to drop in and see that Francis gets in a heap more trouble.

& then go running to the papers to say nothing about their scheme to rob not only poor Gracie but hundreds of others as well, successfully pinning the whole thing on me – with everyone knowing you couldn't believe a word out of their mouths.

Not that that mattered to the papers, of course, with their stupid 'lonely widows' and stuff brought up that ought to have been dead and buried years ago – about Philip's mother and all the rest.

& which, of course, made the crime gang look good.

& who, in the end, got off with a suspended sentence – with Tattoo-Head swearing that I had tried to stab him.

Which is fine – let him go on saying that.

Yeah, shout it out all over Eastern Europe, see if I care – for me and my pals, we are on our way.

Yes, off on our own long-awaited journey at last – all the way to Lambay Island.

Where all my old pals are going to get such a kick out of seeing me coming bombing along on my own personal Frank Tour.

With that old Troy peeping out of the bag, and the Angel of Dresden tucked safely away in her little bit of tissue.

I've even managed to find myself a carnation – a lovely pink one, looking spiffing along with my polka-dot dicky.

And our little gang coming speeding along the coast road, like a flock of butterflies released out into the blue, & the completed proof of the first big Easter Special waiting here for Fr Ron.

& which I've just this minute finished laying out, commemorating all the various events in my life – &, man, that old Frankie Funny, does it look good. Even if I do say so myself, as they say.

The Big Yaroo
Vol. 1, No. 1

TUESDAY WELD: Often compared to Marilyn Monroe because of her Monroe-like quotes to the press when she arrived in Hollywood at fourteen, she is now, at twenty, to prove she's an actress, not a sexpot; currently has her best role to date in *Soldier in the Rain*. But that little girl face atop the curvy chassis.

THE GREAT BRIDGNORTH STAMP APPROVAL AFFAIR, 1958

You can imagine my amazement when, after two whole weeks on the hunt for my booklet – it had actually turned up under a great pile of woodchips in the chicken house – looking a bit the worse for wear, I'm afraid. But I had the solution! Feeling mighty crestfallen, I can tell you, when I finally got back to the house and my bedroom, & opened up my Bridgnorth approvals book for further inspection – before finding, to my dismay, that nearly every single page was ruined, destroyed with blobs of brown-and-white chicken dung.

I felt like such a fool as I turned each sorry-looking page! Until, as the light began, finally, to fail outside, I somehow eventually summoned up the courage to sneak downstairs and commandeer my mother's iron.

And set about smoothing each page with great care – yes, one by one, trying my best not to think of that liquorice-black Scotland Yard Wolseley saloon, coming screeching around the corner, clanging its bell – with, at times, my efforts proving so arduous that I came close to collapsing from a mixture of effort and complete anxiety. Much to my embarrassment, I am forced to confess that, at the very least, I succeeded in burning the back of my hand three times.

Phew.

Our Life in Pictures — Say Hello to the Blanchflowers!
With additional commentary by their friend and fellow sportsman, Jimmy Greaves.

Featuring this week's special:
Match of the Dead

There had, understandably, been a lot of bad feeling about Jimmy Greaves having been omitted from the World Cup squad selected to face Russia in the forthcoming vital game at Wembley Stadium.

With both Blanchflowers having gone on record as stating that whenever the tournament was at last concluded, they would have one or two words that they'd like to share with England's so-called manager – in fact, missing no opportunity that was presented to them in making their displeasure with Alf Ramsey more than evident.

One of them had even threatened to chin him, Uncle Alo had confided in me – as the two of us stood there, together, in the stand.

Mrs Purcell was there too – although don't ask me why.

–It looks like rain, she said – reaching down to retrieve her folded umbrella out of her bag.

And putting it up, as she stared straight ahead.

Dr Roche was present too, and for some reason he was trembling.

Such a silly, I thought, & on such an important, momentous occasion.

I couldn't believe it when I heard the dog barking – at first, I thought it was Mrs Beacon's new fellow – with it turning out to be Grouse Monaghan, from Number 3, The Terrace, long ago.

Uncle Alo was livid about Lev Yashin – the Russian goal-keeper who, by now, was already legendary.

Standing there, tall, like a shadow, in the goalmouth – from head to toe, attired completely in black.

–Without Greavsie, against Lev, we don't stand a chance, he said. This is terrible, really terrible, he added, consuming one Silvermint after the other.

It wasn't long before the game finally began.

With everything seeming to go reasonably well until Ray Wilson sustained an ankle injury.

And that had delayed things for a while – until one of the team foolishly handled the ball in his own penalty area, and that seemed to signal danger for the Russians.

Which it did, in fact – except not in a way that might have been anticipated.

As the ref went over and gave the tall goalkeeper a nudge – after seeing him, like everyone else, inexplicably lying down in the goalmouth.

–*Hold on a minute!* they heard him say – standing there on the goal line, looking around him. This man's dead!

With the strange thing being – that there wasn't so much as sound on the terraces.

No reaction of any kind.

Not a stir.

Even when he said it again.

–*This man's dead!*

Neither did it seem to bother my uncle either – as I stared at Alo's pale, bloodless hands.

Then *pheep!* went the ref, making all sorts of panic-stricken signals.

–*Pheep!* he went again.

Before deciding to make one desperate, hopeful effort.

–PHEEP! went the whistle as he surged forward towards the fourteen-yard line, head down with his arms outstretched.

–PHEEP! it went again. Oh! It's beautiful! he bayed ecstatically. Still nobody moved.

As he cried out again, striking the air as he appealed for all he was worth – just like they used to in the front lounge of the Tower Bar, every single Saturday night.

And which I reminded Uncle Alo of, as we stood there.

But he didn't seem to hear me.

With those same shrill peals of triumph and, just as often, dismay – along with those brief, gladiatorial trumpet blasts – the opening bars of *Match of the Day*.

Do you remember the night we were in there, Uncle Alo? I said, when you were home for a week on your holidays? Man Utd were against Spurs – & Nobby Stiles had played a blinder.

Nobby Stiles, said Uncle Alo – staring straight ahead, with all of the Silvermints now gone, his jaws unmoving:

–Nobby Stiles is playing a blinder.

–Nobby Stiles is playing a blinder, said Alo.

–Alo is playing a blinder, said Nobby.

As, far away, two officials appeared from the tunnel bearing a stretcher.

And Grouse Monaghan barked – as Mrs Purcell made her way towards the exit – somewhat shyly, hunched underneath her umbrella.

As Alo sighed and slipped his hands inside his pockets.

–Nobby is playing a blinder, he said.

–Nobby, you know – he's playing a blinder.

When I looked in the goalmouth, Lev Yashin was gone.

Only, to my amazement, to see – when I turned back, that my father, in his overcoat, had arrived into the stand and was standing by my side.

Smiling as he lifted his wooden rattle–

–except no sound came.

60s special DOWN YOUR WAY (With Saucy Bunn) Inc. reminiscences of early evening rambles in the countryside, funny incidents pertaining to Juke Box Jury, the sounds and impressions of Miss Saucy Bunn, formerly of Hendon, North

London, UK, and her associations with many of the popular groups of the time. Miss Bunn's favourite dessert is sherry trifle and she admits to liking Cliff, just a little. She comes to visit the town every year, and says that 'although it's, at times, a little small' she wouldn't miss both it and Duffy's Circus for the world. Saucy's favourite record hit of the moment, she tells us, is Zager & Evans' 'In the Year 2525', in which the performer paints a picture of a nightmarish future. Is that what it's going to be like, do you think? With jetpacks, flying cars, protein pills and mail delivery by parachute being the order of the day — or is it just a lot of old silly nonsense? We ask Saucy B. (real name Fiona Murtagh).

*This item also references local farmer and beet-grower Wee Pat Casey & his wife Trixie-Mae, formerly of the parish of Drung — & the many and varied 'astonishments' of snow.

Gonks Go Beat (introduced by Saucy Bunn)
This is a musical fantasy film directed by Robert Hartford-Davis, & starring Kenneth Connor and Frank Thornton. Saucy says it is one the great fab films so far of the sixties & no one living in the town should miss it. The story is loosely based on the play *Romeo and Juliet* & features sixteen musical numbers performed by a variety of artists, including Lulu & The Luvvers, the Nashville Teens and members of the Graham

Bond Organisation including Ginger Baker, Jack Bruce and Dick Heckstall-Smith. Do not, under any circumstances, miss this fine film about hip and trendy people who live in a place called Beatland and who all have long hair and jumpers and jeans and sunglasses and listen to cool beat music. Like us ha ha.

CONFECTIONERY THROUGH THE AGES

You tell us! Selected items through the ages include Lucky Lumps, Cough-No-Mores and Clarnico-Murray Choffees.

MY MOST UNFORGETTABLE CHARACTER

All of these stories have one thing in common — somehow each of the characters featured struck home in the memory of the storyteller. Who is yours?

(Next ish: ARE FRIENDS ELECTRIC? Well — some of them sure are, as the well-known international record producer, Thomas Weaver, now based permanently in London, brings us on a trip down memory lane and lifts the lid on what it was like to be a struggling young songwriter in that city in the early seventies, and reveals the background to his cult psychedelic-folk hit, 'Don't Turn off My Soul, Mr Spaceman' — dedicated to his 'lady' of the time, now his wife, and mother to their four beautiful children — Jennifer Junie 'The Moon' McIntyre. Don't miss!)

CANCERTASTROPHE

My diary. With those dastardly old gooseberry-sized spore-distributing aquamen piloting downstream relentlessly once again in their flippers and goggles and visors, making very little sound as they glide determinedly through the heart's arterial branch work, with corpuscles floating through coral caverns like something between a patch of light and a giant jellyfish.

The question is: will they succeed?

RADIO CORNER
(The Wonderful World of Wireless)

Ah, yes — times have certainly changed since the internet, & that's for sure — with very few people bothering to listen to the old radio now. In these go-ahead times when you can even get people to print you a gun. What — print me a gun, do I hear you say? Yes indeed, and probably not very expensive either.

Which is quite a long way from the wooden box in the corner and the shadows swirl around that little gold bead as it twinges and you can hear your father snoring before he wakes up. Yes, before he wakes and says to you:

—Francie. Ah yes, me auld son, what do the likes of you and me care about approvals, or Winston Churchill or anything else? Because there's nothing wrong with the British so there's not. So why wouldn't we listen to the BBC? Turn it up there, Francie — there's a good lad!

Morecambe and Wise
Double Trouble

The Kaye Sisters
Three in Harmony
Jimmy Clitheroe
The Clitheroe Kid
Ted Lune
Lancashire's Long Laugh
Peter Sinclair
Cock O' the North
Margo Henderson
Impressions at the Piano
The Demijeans
Two Boys and A Girl
–Oh, man alive, but them's great programmes, he said.
–Tune the dial, our boy, and find me some more.

Oh, do you know the muffin man
The muffin man, the muffin man
Do you know the muffin man
Who lives in Drury Lane?

As back he went in the armchair in his braces and baggy brown suit, sipping patiently from his bottle of Guinness.

& then, out it swept, his all-time favourite: 'High Adventure', the opening theme from the weekly music programme *Friday Night Is Music Night*.

As he sighed and released a contented moan and began to softly hum along with the melody – holding my hand as the music of the orchestra seemed to drift out from the baize in green and blue waves, ascending fluidly high above the town – and, indeed, the entire country, returning to the far foreign ports of their origin, there to twinkle on the other side of the world.

–It's OK, Francie. It's OK now. That's all, my son, that you've got to remember.

–And now we present *Sing Something Simple*, continued the compère, prevailing on us to accompany him inside the interior of that polished wooden cabinet, enter in his company into that reassuring world of glowing ochre – yes, glide from the comfort of our humble lamplit kitchen into the vast and magic night-city that we'd renamed World of Wireless.

Maybe in another dimension, in a Dan Dare-style universe complete with shimmering rooftops of domed valves and gleamingly lyrical capillary wires, with a magnetic dial-hand scanning a velvet-blue, flickering sky, I considered, deep inside of which, behind that warm, chevron-grille wave cloth, my father could perhaps have been a presenter of his very own late-night programme.

–Good evening. This is Francie Brady's father – and tonight we focus on our boy's special favourite – The Q Bikes.

EDITOR'S ROUNDUP

Yes, even those old stripy twins somehow don't seem to bother me any more, I'm happy to be able to say – as a matter of fact every time I think of them I find myself, willingly, back in Grace Courtney's shop, which was where, of course, I had first encountered them, reposing in all their majestic glory in an elaborate gilt frame just above the fanlight of that old four-storey Georgian house.

–The pride of Haberdashers'! she had always used to call them, my proud heroes of the Upper Third!

&, though the two chaps themselves might not have been actually physically present in the church this morning, let there be no doubt whatsoever but you could sense their warmth and solidarity all around you – bathing you in an otherworldly haze – what would once have been described as a 'state of grace'.

& I'd heard one of them say – don't ask me which, for to this very day I've never been able to tell them apart.

—You're not, in fact, a pig, Mr Brady – and never were. We only said that for a laugh. &, on behalf of my brother and myself, I would be privileged if you would accept our apology.

As I closed my eyes and folded my hands – just the very same as I used to when I still believed in Our Lady – and not be surprised when she'd toss you a lovely spring snowdrop with the sweetest, nodding little bone-china head.

LATE EXTRA

If you happened to be trapped in a barn or pumphouse with a black plastic sack pulled down over your head, what action do you think you might take? Would you yell Yaroo! like a certain over-inquisitive gardener — or do you think you'd come up with some alternative, ingenious plan? Well if you did it would be a hell of a lot more than that poor old idiot Scuttler Corrigan has succeeded in doing — at least, not yet. That's it, Corrigan — you just keep on yowling. Because, sooner or later, someone's bound to hear you!

Concept & Editorial: F. Brady
Cover art: F. Brady
Script: F. Brady
Pencils: F Brady
Inks: F. Brady

Yes, so there you have it – that's the magazine. & that, more or less, is all my work done.

Now that I've got everything ready and 'in the bag', to coin a phrase ha ha – with Troy and the angel getting ready to be my guides, along with the bells of Easter Sunday morning.

As I check the magazine, page by page, for mistakes – knowing full well that I'm only being fizzy-neurotic in the head like all of us here in Fizzbag, for God knows how many times I've already double-checked it.

& then delving down into the depths of my pannier bags – just to be certain that Troy had got his cap.

& which he always has – only before I zip up the cover, his small hand closes over my wrist and he lifts himself up and looks me right in the eye.

–I'm sorry I was never really in the house with you & Philip Nugent. You know that, don't you? That there was never any day called *Teatime with Tommy* & you didn't write any composition for the teacher.

&, maybe because I knew in my heart that he meant no harm by what he was saying, I had very little difficulty nodding and agreeing with the diminutive naval officer – thumbing the silvery reflection of my tears from underneath those pink glossy lids as I made clear that that was the case.

–It's true, Troy, I know that. But you have to remember there were other days.

Such as the one me and Joe had spent in the plantin, if you ever heard of it – a place where there's trees but not enough to call a wood – you could get into it by pushing through the briars at the back of the chicken house.

Anyhow, that's where we found ourselves, the two of us – not long after our hide by the river had got filled in by diggers – when a lump of the aqueduct bridge had come loose and fell into it.

–So that's the end of the hide, said Joe, now we'll have to go and find another.

It turned out to be as good as our riverside nook.

–This sure is a swell spot, said Joe, once again The Manitou has done us proud, *kemo sabe.*

–Look after us, Joe, you mean? I said.

–Yup! he agreed, and showed us the way to the happy hunting grounds part two.

Even if it wasn't much more than a long-forgotten rubbish dump – with nothing in it only a pile of nettle-covered bricks, a clump of diseased dog daisies & the broken frame of a bike long since become part of the clay.

But, all the same, this is the spot for us, said Joe – suddenly haring off and scaling up the tallest pine tree like a cat – staring out from a branch, as far as the eye could see.

–There's something I've been meaning to ask you, he says.

As I continued on digging down deep in the earth before discovering an interesting cache of stones – all smooth and round, glittering in the sun.

Which I set aside as I lifted my head – as Joe continued just whittling away.

He always seemed to be carving out catapults.

–If you were trapped on a desert island, he began, if you happened to be trapped on a desert island after a plane crash and one of the passengers had been murdered but you couldn't say which of the survivors had done it – *what would you do?*

I thought for a while, imagining each face – & them all doing their best to seem unconcerned – as if they hadn't a care in the world.

But I couldn't figure it out.

Although I did know this much – and said it to Joe, without even thinking.

That Philip, if he was here, wouldn't be long cracking the case. Coming along with his magnifying glass.

—Probably only be a matter of minutes, I suggested.

—It's a pity he's not, though, I heard Joe saying, here I mean – as he looked down and smiled, with his legs swinging out in front of him.

—Yeah, I reckon. It shore is a pity about that old Philip Nooge, I said.

—I guess that's the way, I heard him reply, as he closed one eye and drew back the elastic of his slingshot.

I'm not even sure where Philip had got to.

Although I think he might have gone to Newtown, which he sometimes did, to his auntie's.

—Of all the towns, this is the best, said Joe.

—You know that, don't you – it's true, ain't it amigo?

Those, more or less, were the last words I remember Joe saying.

& even if I'd wanted to, I couldn't have stopped myself recalling them.

—Because no matter what you done, Francie, you'll always still be one of us. And if anyone asks, that's just the way it is.

As I made my way back over to the window, to check one last time on good old Madame Speedy – who was out there waiting, every bit as good as new, just a bit out of sight in behind the hut.

Yes, one hell of a gleaming flash machine, that's just about the only way I can describe Her Majesty.

With scarcely half an hour left now to go – until the arrival, at last, of busting-out time.

When Frank 'The Q-Bike' Brady finally makes his long-promised getaway.

I've already double- and triple-checked and Fr McGivney is nowhere to be found – having headed off to Carlow, presumably, like he'd promised – & which, of course, had been part of the plan all along.

So, def-in-itely, all is looking good – & a far cry, for sure, from the night of the so-called Russians.

Because I've come a long way since that, I'm afraid.

Still, I suppose, in its way, it was good, in a way, that it happened.

Considering the amount that you learn from these things.

& with nothing, this time, as I say, being left to chance.

In fact, if anything, I might have over-prepared – attired as I am in in this head-to-toe waterproof, maybe running the risk of attracting unwarranted attention.

But, all the same, according to my meteorological charts, there is likely going to be a downpour around lunchtime – at which point I ought to be coming through the village of Swords.

No – no sense in leaving anything to chance.

So, along with my goggles, I'm pretty much all set.

Which I got for a song – unexpectedly, on eBay.

In a special offer with a Biggles-style leatherneck cap, which turned out to be an absolute one hundred per cent perfect fit.

–Now you is one of the X-Men, Old School! laughed Ricky whenever he seen me.

And who, I know, I am really going to miss.

But what's done, as they say, is done – and there can be no going back.

Under any circumstances.

That much I've learned.

Whether from 'Russians' or anyone else.

Yes, make your decision – and stick to it.

That's the only real thing that's important – make sure and do that, and everything else will follow automatically.

Because, no matter what they say, there are just some things that are never going to change – in spite of all these modern developments.

I mean, I was reading, just this morning, when I was preparing my bits and pieces – about this fellow, this amputee in the

States & how, so far as he was concerned, losing all his limbs was the best thing that had ever happened.

And if you don't believe me, he goes on to say, *then all you have to do is ask my wife. Who'll tell you – you see if she doesn't! – who'll tell you that, before all of this happened, that – quite frankly – I used to be a bit of a doom-and-gloom merchant. A bit of a stress-head, really, to be honest.*

Not any more, however, he said, because ever since becoming a quadriplegic he has been transformed into a much much happier man.

With his wife in the photo, smiling away as proud as Punch.

Absolutely and completely true, without question! she says.

&, funny as it is – and I really am sorry to be saying this – maybe it's because my nerves are at me over the trip, but I can't help but wonder if, in a couple of short years, she'll find herself able to say the same thing.

Or will her armless and legless partner of thirty years have turned into a bitter old stump of a thing – arsing around the kitchen complaining about everything, giving out about her being left with all of her arms and legs and him with nothing.

I don't know – I mean, with something like that, how can you be certain?

But I genuinely do hope so – that, limbs or no limbs, the two of them will stay together and remain a happy couple.

For what, in the end, does any of us want?

–Only contentment, as Fr Ron always says, some small measure of satisfaction, that's all, Frank.

& which, I'm delighted to be able to say, in my own life, has been the case – against all the odds, I suppose you might say!

Yes, a profoundly fulfilling & rewarding story – with all the details, warts and all, contained now forever in my copy of *The Big Yaroo*.

Which lies there waiting for anyone who might care to avail of it.

Thanks, mostly, to Fr Ron because of all his advice and expertise with the production of the first and only issue – but also Dr Cecil for his time and wisdom.

Thanks, guys.

A gesture which, I'm afraid I'm sorry to have to say, I can't find within me to extend to Dr Kiernan, the great big squinty-eyed clocking fucking hen – however he managed to get himself appointed head of anything – when he should have been looking after petrol pumps or something.

So, take a bow, both of you – for you were always there by my side when needed.

I can't believe that we've got this far.

Me, the little angel, Captain Troy – &, of course, all my memories.

It's almost impossible to believe, you know?

With all those bells out there ringing out over Dublin City for Easter – & making, as they do, you think of the cover of *Playhour* long ago, with that lop-eared rabbit clapping away with his soft little paws, & his crestfallen face completely covered in lumpy strawberry.

As his put-upon, poor old exasperated mummy once more good-naturedly gives it a wipe and leads him around the kitchen in a dance:

Easter bunny
Looking funny
With his basket of eggs
Bells are ringing
Children singing,
'Hooray for Easter Day!'

With that being the last thing I have time for before going – because, like I say, I can't afford to take risks.

& have to stick exactly to the plan.

As I sit down and type *The Big Yaroo*'s final words.

```
Hi everyone
I just want to say that it was nice to have
been here in Fizzbag this last fifty years and
how I'm just sorry now I have to go. I would
also like to offer my apologies for everything
that I've done in the past and for you to
know that I am deeply regretful for having
harmed my innocent neighbour in the cruel and
thoughtless way that I did and that if there
was anything I could do to make it not be
that way any more then that is what I would
definitely do. The staff have really been very
good to me here over the years and I would
like to express my special gratitude to them.
    With every good wish
    I remain
    Yours sincerely
    The Editor
    The Big Yaroo
```

With my best-laid plan nearly coming asunder even before I'd finished – when the door of the shed burst open, and who arrives in only Shabs, waving his mobile – before giving me this almighty belter in the ribs, shouting about the CIA and–

–What is you doing wearing that helmet? he says.

As I pressed my finger against my lips.

–*Sssh!* I said – and away he goes, with the door swinging behind him.

What a character.

Beside the computer, I've left Mrs Beacon a thank-you card.

As a token of the days we'd spent in Blanch – when, together, we'd discovered that the game was finally up.

With them old Gonks of Bad, those long-feared aquanauts of evil having succeeded in making it as far as my brain.

And it's hard not to think about – as it is her, and what might become of her, if I do actually go.

Break out, I mean.

–I love my little doggie so much, she had told me, every bit as much as poor old Toddy Ray – & which I never thought I would. It breaks my heart to even leave him for an hour – & why I'm so grateful to you for taking him out for walks, Frank. I pray to God nothing ever happens to him.

She's a lovely woman – the best there ever was.

And which is why, the more I think of it, the greater the anxiety becomes that something – some awful tragedy, for God knows there are plenty out there – might somehow befall either her or her new pet.

Or both, God forbid.

& that is why, as so often before, I can feel that lump beginning to swell again in my throat.

& I hold up the letter that I've written and slowly begin to sob.

–Because I know it just wouldn't be fair, I say – as I gradually, deliberately, begin shredding it into tiny little pieces.

Accepting that, in the end, it would be better, and fairer, to leave my planned Great Escape until Easter Sunday of next year – or perhaps even the Monday.

Because, after all, let's face it – there's enough lonely people, isn't there, in the world.

And – who knows? Maybe by then the aquanauts might have decided to turn back – or, at the very least, temporarily suspend their advances.

Mrs Beacon says it's possible.

& how wonderful that would be, with Fr Ron saying:

–*You're Lazarus, Frank!*

& we could all stay here together, not being worried any more about anything.

Until the day comes when we're all, contented, lying in the churchyard together – with none of us being in the least bit bothered.

Because I guess we'll know we've done our best – as we embark on the greatest breakout ever, where they'll all be waiting for us patiently – The Prof and all the rest who, over the years, have passed through the gates of Fizzbag.

But, most of all, a certain inch-high couple squealing and cavorting against the spray – with, the second my mother sees me, the atomic eruption of her cry irradiating the Pacific sky:

–I cannot believe it – after all this time! Just where on earth have you been, Bunny Cuddles?

The End